PARINEETA

Saratchandra Chattopadhyay was born on 15 September 1876 in Devanandapur, a village in West Bengal. He grew up in dire poverty and received very little formal education. After spending some of his youth in Bhagalpur and Muzaffarpur, Saratchandra left for Burma in 1903, and it was from Burma that he began to send his stories and novels to magazines in Kolkata. Sensitive and daring, Saratchandra's writings captivated the hearts and minds of readers, and he soon became Bengal's most popular novelist. Saratchandra returned to Kolkata in 1916, and dedicated himself to writing. He was India's first successful professional writer—a person who earned his entire livelihood only from writing. He died in 1938.

Saratchandra remains one of the best-loved Indian novelists of all time; his works have been translated into various languages and made into films as well. Among his best-known novels are *Srikanta*, *Devdas*, *Palli Samaj*, *Parineeta*, *Charitraheen*, *Grihadaha* and *Pather Dabi*.

*

Malobika Chaudhuri runs Mono Translation Bureau, a multi-lingual translation agency, in Kolkata. Her translations of several of Saratchandra's novels are forthcoming.

*

Swagato Ganguly has a PhD in Comparative Literature and Literary Theory from University of Pennsylvania.

Parineeta

SARATCHANDRA CHATTOPADHYAY

Translated from the Bengali by
MALOBIKA CHAUDHURI

Introduction by
SWAGATO GANGULY

PENGUIN BOOKS

PENGUIN BOOKS
Published by the Penguin Group
Penguin Books India Pvt. Ltd, 11 Community Centre, Panchsheel Park, New Delhi 110 017, India
Penguin Group (USA) Inc., 375 Hudson Street, New York, New York 10014, USA
Penguin Group (Canada), 10 Alcorn Avenue, Toronto, Ontario, Canada M4V 3B2 (a division of Pearson Penguin Canada Inc.)
Penguin Books Ltd, 80 Strand, London WC2R 0RL, England
Penguin Ireland, 25 St Stephen's Green, Dublin 2, Ireland (a division of Penguin Books Ltd)
Penguin Group (Australia), 250 Camberwell Road, Camberwell, Victoria 3124, Australia (a division of Pearson Australia Group Pty Ltd)
Penguin Group (NZ), cnr Airborne and Rosedale Roads, Albany, Auckland 1310, New Zealand (a division of Pearson New Zealand Ltd)
Penguin Group (South Africa) (Pty) Ltd, 24 Sturdee Avenue, Rosebank, Johannesburg 2196, South Africa

Penguin Books Ltd, Registered Offices: 80 Strand, London WC2R 0RL, England

First published by Penguin Books India 2005
This translation copyright © Penguin Books India 2005
Introduction copyright © Penguin Books India 2005

Typeset in *Perpetua* by Mantra Virtual Services, New Delhi
Printed at Chaman Offset Printer.

INTRODUCTION

When in a crucial scene of this early novella by Saratchandra Chattopadhyay Lalita garlands Shekhar and Shekhar reciprocates, it becomes what linguists have called a performative act—the exchange of garlands is not just symbolic of a Hindu marriage, it *is* the marriage. Thereafter Lalita has to live with the consequences of that gesture, which includes refusing her lover and benefactor Girin even though Shekhar spurns her. If one remembers that Lalita is only fourteen, her seemingly innocent act of garlanding Shekhar at a cousin's doll's wedding presents an enigma of teenage sexuality reminiscent of her well-known namesake in world literature—Vladimir Nabokov's Lolita. And Shekhar is like Humbert Humbert too, driven by a passion for Lalita where desire and disgust intermingle. The difference with Nabokov's Lolita, though, is that once having undertaken a certain ritual act Lalita is constrained to bear the burden of that act until misunderstandings are resolved, Shekhar sees the error of his ways, and accepts her as his lawfully wedded wife.

To understand the novella in the context of its time a bit of social history is essential: child marriages were the norm during much of Saratchandra Chattopadhyay's lifetime (1876-1938), and did not attract any penalties from the law at the time of *Parineeta*'s publication in 1914. Saratchandra Chattopadhyay was born into a poor Brahmin family in the small village of Devanandapur in Bengal, but their poverty was alleviated somewhat by Saratchandra's wealthy maternal grandfather, who took the family under his wing. The family fortunes dwindled, however, when the grandfather died in 1892, and deteriorated further with Saratchandra's mother's death in 1895. Saratchandra, who took after his bohemian father, left the family soon thereafter, and alternated between petty jobs and living the life of a wandering ascetic. He revealed an affinity for society's lower depths, perhaps as an escape from the hypocrisies of a shabby-genteel existence. Having become a man of ill repute he moved from Bengal to Burma, where he stayed for over a decade and worked at clerical jobs. The novels he composed during this period, which included *Parineeta* (Espoused) and other classics such as *Devdas* and *Charitraheen* (The Immoralist), made him wildly popular as they trickled back to Kolkata.

The beginning of the twentieth century witnessed, in fact, a rapid expansion of literary periodicals and of the reading public in Bengal, comparable to the explosion in television channels today. This enabled Saratchandra to become the first successful professional writer in India, and by the time he was in his forties he was making a comfortable living from his writing alone. While he was well attuned to the requirements of his reading public, what saved his writing from becoming the equivalent of today's televised soap operas was the realism and wide social sympathy that it expressed. Saratchandra, along with contemporary literary giant Rabindranath Tagore, was among the first to give women a voice in his novels. But their outlooks couldn't be more different in many respects. A wealthy landlord, Tagore penned lofty and metaphysical novels, and developed an attitude ˜critical of the mass nationalism that swept the country in the 1920s and 1930s. Saratchandra, scion of the lower middle class, wrote novels that were more earthy and attuned to popular sentiment, and his pro-revolutionary *Pather Dabi* (Call of the Road) was banned by the British when it was published in 1926.

As a love story *Parineeta* might seem formulaic, but it was among the initiators of the genre of the romantic novel in India, set against the backdrop of extraordinary prohibitions and restraints on contact between the sexes. Love must find its way through indirection, and a recurrent motif in Saratchandra's fiction is romance between men suffering from a lingering and prolonged illness and women who nurse them back to health, a throwback to the primary Oedipal situation with women cast in a maternal role. Another common pattern is that of the lovers playing together as children and practically growing up together, close to the scenario in *Parineeta* where the action takes place between families who have been next-door neighbours for a long time.

The concern with respectability means that, as in a Jane

Austen novel, characters are suspended between romance and finance, even though in Austenian terms Saratchandra might seem too full of sensibility. *Parineita* has a classic rich boy–poor girl plot line where Lalita has been Shekhar's helpmeet for quite some time, but marriage between them is out of the question. Lalita is an orphan, and Gurucharan, her uncle and guardian, is a clerk ruined by having to marry off too many daughters; while Shekhar's father Nabin Roy is a successful businessman on the prowl for a large dowry for his son. The narrative turns on the irony that is implicit in Shekhar's inability to own up to his desires and gestures regarding Lalita:

> It was a fact that he could not marry Lalita without his parents' consent. However, if the cause for her marriage to Girin not taking place were made public, how would he be able to handle all the gossip that would reverberate all around?

In Austen's novels the balance between romance and respectability is finely maintained till the end, while Saratchandra causes romance to win out when Shekhar, shamed by Lalita's steadfastness and Girin's sacrifice in not taking advantage of his plight, cancels the rich marriage that was being planned for him and acknowledges his tie to Lalita.

Compared to the heroes of Tagore's fiction, who are mostly serious and reflective people, Saratchandra's heroes act on impulse and can appear vacillating, indecisive, even petulant. While the men manifest a certain emotional indiscipline, women are subjected to a ritual discipline that leaves them slightly demented, representing various shades of the Victorian 'madwoman in the attic' syndrome, as it were. Saratchandra, in fact, brings us closer to the Bengali middle class of his time, subjected at once to colonial disciplinarity, conservative social norms, and the romantic desire to escape. A common theme in his novels is sacrifice, which sublimates desire and acts as a redemptive force. Women most often have to bear the burden of that sacrifice. Thus Lalita puts her entire life on the stake, and gives up Girin who wants to marry her, because Shekhar had once enacted the Hindu rite of marriage with her even if he disowns her afterwards. But Saratchandra speaks equally eloquently of the discontents of that sacrifice, which is the source of the ambivalence in his heroes as well as his stories. Thus the normally humble and submissive Gurucharan gives up the Hindu religion altogether in a fit of revolt, embracing the Brahmo creed instead; and Saratchandra's narrative implies that he might have good reasons for doing so, having been ruined by the dowry he has to pay for his daughters as well as by the avaricious Nabin Roy who takes his stand by conservative Hinduism.

This ambivalent amalgam of the conservative and the provocative is a staple of Saratchandra's fiction, and manifests itself at many levels in *Parineeta*. The title itself, instead of incorporating, as that of Nabokov's novel does, the name of the lively and spirited heroine at the center of the narrative, is austerely structural—'espoused: a married woman'. Nabin Roy, the father figure, has to be killed off before Shekhar can formally acknowledge his tie to Lalita. Even in the case of Bhuvaneshwari, his sympathetic mother, Shekhar does suggest that Lalita seek her blessings when they exchange garlands, but keeps mum about the marriage for years afterwards.

Significantly, despite Shekhar taking the lead in all aspects of the relationship with Lalita, it is Lalita who makes the first move when they exchange garlands. She scarcely knows what she does when the conch shells of Annakali's doll's wedding sound, but it is as if her unconscious speaks while, as in the case of Freud's adolescent subject Dora in his *An Analysis of a Case of Hysteria*, repressed wishes and desires emerge as bodily symptoms: 'a shiver of some unknown feeling ran through Lalita's entire body'.

Not only has Saratchandra's work been translated into all the major Indian languages and proven amenable to stage and screen adaptations in many of these languages, his popularity has endured from the moment his novels started to be serialized in the leading Bengali periodicals of its day, upto the present. Nobody has plumbed the depths of the twentieth century Bengali middle class psyche quite like him, but it is fair to say that his appeal is pan-Indian. The ambivalence of his characters is, at bottom, the ambivalence felt by tradition-bound individuals cast adrift, yet also paradoxically empowered, by a slowly but irrevocably modernizing society. This pathos doubtless accounts for his easy translatability into other Indian languages, as well as other media such as theatre and film. It is no surprise that Bollywood, the mainstream Hindi cinema, has found Saratchandra very conducive, lapping up his novels ever since it got into the business of talkies, and even before (a silent version of *Devdas* was shot as early as 1928). *Parineeta* was filmed by Bimal Roy, master of neo-realism, in 1953. Half a century later it has been adapted for the screen once again by filmmaker Vidhu Vinod Chopra, evidence that the work is still fresh and continues to find new interpretations.

Kolkata
February 2005

Swagato Ganguly

IF A THUNDERBOLT HAD STRUCK HIM DOWN, HE WOULD have undoubtedly experienced searing pain. But the agony reflected on Gurucharan's visage was probably far greater when, right in the morning, he was brought the news that his wife had safely delivered their fifth girl child.

Gurucharan was a petty bank clerk with a salary of sixty rupees. He had the appearance of a man who was all shrivelled up, whose mind had withered away. His demeanour too seemed to reflect an impassive and uninvolved attitude. Even then, this ominous good news froze the hookah in his hand and all that he could do was to lean back weakly on the ancient pillow. There was no energy in him to even release the pent up deep sigh.

The joyful news had been heralded by his ten-year-old daughter Annakali. She said, 'Baba, won't you come and take a look?'

Looking up at his daughter, Gurucharan said, 'Just fetch me a glass of water, dear.'

Annakali left to get the water. As she went out, Gurucharan's mind raced through all the expenses involved in the delivery. Then, in the manner of train passengers of the third class who with all their belongings of various shapes and sizes cause a stampede in their efforts to bustle in through the door—innumerable worries and problems began to flood in. He remembered that the previous year, on the auspicious occasion of his second daughter's marriage, this two-storeyed house of his in Bowbazar had been mortgaged and that the interest for the last six months was also overdue. Only a month or so remained before the festive season started and gifts would have to be sent to the in-laws of yet another daughter. Yesterday in the office, in spite of working till 8 p.m., he had been unable to balance the debit and credit columns in the ledger; and it was mandatory to send the accounts to England by noon. Further, his superior had laid down the stern injunction that dirty and unkempt clothes could not be worn to office on pain of a fine. But since last week, the washerwoman had presumably disappeared—along with half the clothes of the household.

Now, Gurucharan felt as if he did not have the strength to even lean back against the pillow. Raising the hookah aloft he crumpled onto the bed. He thought to himself, 'Dear God, so many people are crushed to death in the traffic of Kolkata every day; in your eyes are they even greater sinners than I am? Almighty, show some mercy towards me, can't some vehicle run over me?'

None in the family noticed the deep-rooted agony of the careworn, battered man, overburdened and aged beyond his years.

Handing him the water Annakali said, 'Baba, get up,

here is the water.'

Sitting up, Gurucharan gulped down the water in one breath and said, 'Ahh! Go on, dear, take away the glass.'

Once she left, Gurucharan lay back on the pillow again.

Entering the room Lalita said, 'Mama, I have brought tea, get up.'

On hearing that tea had been brought, Gurucharan sat up once again. Looking at Lalita, he felt soothed and half his problems seemed to melt away. Affectionately Gurucharan said, 'You have kept a vigil all night, come and sit here, next to me.'

Lalita said with a soft smile, 'I did not stay awake all night, Mama.'

Gurucharan answered, 'That does not matter, come close to me.'

Lalita sat down beside him, and Gurucharan placing his hand on her head suddenly remarked aloud, 'If only I could marry this blessed child of mine into an appropriately prosperous family, it would be a truly worthwhile achievement.'

With bowed head Lalita poured the tea as Gurucharan continued, 'My dear, you have to labour very hard all the time in your poor Mama's household, don't you?'

Lalita shook her head, 'Why do you feel that only I work all the time, Mama? Everybody works and so do I.'

Now Gurucharan smiled, 'So, Lalita, tell me, who will be taking care of the cooking today?'

Looking up she answered, 'Why Mama, I will manage!'

Surprised, Gurucharan could only respond, 'How will you manage, my dear? Do you even know how to cook?'

'I do know, Mama. I have picked up everything from Mami.'

Putting down the tea cup Gurucharan said, 'Really?'

'Oh yes! Mami has often shown me what to do and, having learnt so much from her, I have done the cooking on so many occasions,' saying which Lalita lowered her head once again. Laying his hand on her head, Gurucharan silently blessed her. One giant burden regarding the running of the house seemed to lift from his mind.

Gurucharan's room opened on to the alley. Sipping tea and looking out, he suddenly called out loudly, 'Shekhar, is that you? Just step in for a moment.'

A tall, handsome and well-built young man came in.

Gurucharan said, 'You have heard what your Khurima has done this morning?'

Smiling gently Shekhar answered, 'What has she done? You are referring to the birth of your daughter, aren't you?'

Sighing heavily, Gurucharan responded, 'You too talk about this so casually, Shekhar; only I know what this really means.'

'Don't talk in that manner, Kaka, Khurima will be very upset. Besides, whomever the Almighty has sent should be welcomed with joy.'

After remaining silent for a while, Gurucharan replied, 'I also know that one ought to celebrate! But, young man, even God has not been very fair. I am poor, why so much bounty in my household? Even this very house has been mortgaged to your father—but that does not matter, it does not upset me in the least. But, just think of this—this orphan, this Lalita of mine—this golden child is only fit for royalty. How do I give her away in marriage to just anybody? If innumerable jewels like the Kohinoor that grace the crown were heaped together, they would still fall short when compared to my child. However, who will appreciate that? Sheer penury will force me to give away this rare gem to someone who is unworthy of her. Tell me, doesn't it tear one's heart apart to think of such circumstances? She is all of thirteen years old and I do not have thirteen coins to my name to even look for a suitable match for her.'

Gurucharan's eyes brimmed over with tears. Shekhar remained silent. Gurucharan said once again, 'Shekharnath, just look around in your circle of friends. Maybe something can be done for this girl. I have heard that there are some boys who don't think so much of money or dowry, but take into consideration only the girl herself. If somehow you could find someone like that ... I am telling you Shekhar, my blessings will make you the king of kings. What else can I say? It is because of your family's patronage that I live in the neighbourhood. Your father looks on me as a younger brother.'

Shekhar nodded in agreement.

Gurucharan continued, 'Don't forget, my boy, keep it in mind. Ever since she turned eight Lalita has been studying and growing up under your guidance. You have seen for yourself what an intelligent, sensitive and disciplined girl she is. Just a slip of a child and from today it is she who will be doing all the cooking, serving— everything is in her hands.'

At this moment Lalita looked up once and lowered her eyes immediately. Her lips quivered slightly. Gurucharan continued with a sigh, 'Did her father earn any less! But he gave away all his property in such a manner that nothing remains, even for this one child.'

Shekhar did not say anything. Yet again Gurucharan spoke aloud, 'But then, how can I say he did not leave her anything? The blessings of the people whose miseries he helped wipe away have all seeped deep into her. Or else, how could such a young child assume the form of a Bountiful Mother! Is that true or not, Shekhar?'

Smiling, Shekhar did not respond.

On seeing him about to leave Gurucharan asked, 'Where are you off to so early?'

Shekhar answered, 'To the barrister—there is a case.' As he stood up, Gurucharan reminded him once again, 'Just keep what I have said in mind! She is a bit dark, but such a pretty face and so much love and caring cannot be found in a person anywhere else on earth.'

Nodding, Shekhar left with a smile. He was about twenty-five. Since the completion of his Master's degree he had been teaching, and only the previous year had qualified as an attorney. His father, Nabin Roy, who had made millions in the jaggery trade, had given up active business and now concentrated on money lending from the house itself. His elder son was Abinash the attorney; Shekharnath was the younger one. Their gigantic three-storeyed house stood at the head of the street and a large open terrace allowed easy access and communication between his house and Gurucharan's; hence an intimacy had rapidly grown between the two families. The women of the household often used this route to communicate and keep in touch.

2

A MATRIMONIAL ALLIANCE FOR SHEKHAR HAD BEEN proposed from a wealthy family of Shyambazar; the matter had been under discussion for some time now. The other day, the prospective bride's family had come over for a visit and today they wanted to appoint an appropriately auspicious day in the coming winter for the marriage. Naturally, it was up to Shekhar's parents to confirm their interest first. Shekhar's mother Bhuvaneshwari, however, did not consent. She sent word with the maid-servant, 'Only when the boy chooses a bride for himself will I get my son married and not otherwise.'

Nabin Roy was unhappy with this complicated logic of his wife. He was focussed only on the monetary benefits of this alliance and was irked that his wife should have such a flippant outlook. 'What sense does that make?' he said irritatedly. 'We have already had a look at the girl. Let us confirm an engagement—and the formalities can then be finalized on an appropriately auspicious day.'

Bhuvaneshwari knew that her husband was displeased. Still, she refused to consent to a formal engagement. In a display of anger, Nabin Roy had his meal very late that day and even took his afternoon siesta in the outer room.

One evening, about five to six days later, Lalita entered the plushly decorated room that belonged to Shekhar. He was standing in front of the large mirror, preparing himself to go out for the inspection of a prospective bride. Silently looking on for a while, she asked, 'Are you going out to choose a bride?'

Turning around, Shekhar said, 'Ah, there you are! Help me to dress such that my bride chooses me!'

Lalita laughed and responded, 'I don't have time today, Shekhar da—I have just come for some money.' She then proceeded to take the keys of his cupboard from under the pillow, and opening the drawer, took some notes which she tied to one end of her sari, saying to herself, 'I am taking money whenever I need it, but how will it all be repaid?'

Carefully brushing his hair into a particular style, Shekhar replied, 'It will not be repaid Lalita, on the contrary it is being repaid.'

Not understanding, Lalita looked on blankly.

'You don't understand?'

Lalita shook her head, 'No!'

'Grow up a little more and you will,' saying which Shekhar put on his shoes and left.

That night Shekhar was stretched out on the couch when his mother entered the room. He sat up quickly. Sitting at one end of the couch she asked, 'And how did you find the girl?'

Looking at his mother affectionately, Shekhar answered, 'Fine!'

Bhuvaneshwari was nearly fifty, but had kept herself so well that she did not look a day over thirty-five. Further, the maternal heart that beat in her bosom was evergreen and ever tender. She came from a rustic background; she had been born and brought up in a village——but even in an urban setting she did not appear out of place for even a day. Just as easily as she accepted the vibrant, pulsating life of the city, she also kept in touch with the calmness and sweetness of her birthplace. Just how proud Shekhar was of such an outstanding mother, perhaps Bhuvaneshwari herself did not have any idea. The Almighty had blessed Shekhar with a lot——sturdy good health, good looks, youth and intelligence; but it was being his mother's son that he regarded wholeheartedly as being the biggest boon of all.

Presently his mother said, 'Wonderful, you remain silent after making such a remark!'

Once again with a smile Shekhar responded, 'Well, I did answer your question.'

Bhuvaneshwari too smiled and said, 'What sort of answer was that? Tell me, is she dark or fair? Whom does she resemble? Our Lalita?'

Looking up Shekhar replied, 'Lalita is dark, this girl is fairer.'

'And her features?'

'Not bad.'

'Then, should I talk to your father?'

Shekhar remained silent.

Looking at her son for a couple of minutes, Bhuvaneshwari finally asked, 'What about her education? How far has she studied?'

'I did not think of asking,' Shekhar replied.

His mother exclaimed, 'You did not think of asking! You did not ask about a matter which has become the most important factor these days?!'

Shekhar laughed and said, 'No Ma, the thought did not even occur to me.'

Amazed at her son's reply, Bhuvaneshwari stared at him for a while and then, laughing aloud exclaimed, 'That means you have no interest in marrying her!'

Shekhar was about to say something but seeing Lalita enter the room, fell silent. Lalita walked in steadily and took a post behind Bhuvaneshwari's chair. Extending her left hand Bhuvaneshwari brought her forward and asked, 'What is it, my dear?'

Quietly Lalita answered, 'Nothing, Ma.'

Earlier Lalita used to address Bhuvaneshwari as 'Mashima', but, one day forbidding her to do so Bhuvaneshwari had said, 'I am no aunt of yours, Lalita, I'm your mother.' Ever since, Lalita had addressed her as 'Ma'.

Pulling her even closer, Bhuvaneshwari affectionately asked, 'Nothing at all? Then I suppose you have come just to have a look at me!'

Shekhar questioned, 'Has come to see you? But isn't she supposed to be cooking in her Mama's house?'

'But why should she cook at all?' asked his mother.

Surprised, Shekhar responded, 'Who else will do the cooking in that house? Even her uncle said the other day that she would have to see to the cooking and all the housework now.'

Bhuvaneshwari laughed aloud, 'Her uncle! What he said then is hardly relevant. She is not even married as yet—who will eat what she has cooked? She need not get bothered by all that. I have sent over our Brahmin cook, that lady will see to everything. Your sister-in-law is doing our cooking, so there's no need to worry about food and such matters.'

It was apparent to Shekhar that his mother had taken on herself the responsibility of easing the heavy burdens of their poverty-stricken neighbours; he released a sigh of relief.

A month passed by. One day as Shekhar lay stretched out on his couch Lalita entered his room. Extracting the bunch of keys, she rather noisily opened the cupboard drawer. Without raising his eyes from the book, Shekhar asked, 'What?'

Lalita answered, 'I am taking money.'

'Hmm!' said Shekhar and continued to read. Knotting the money at one end of her sari Lalita stood up. She had made quite an effort in dressing up that day and wanted Shekhar to notice. She said, 'I have taken ten rupees,

Shekhar da.'

'Fine,' said Shekhar, without looking up from his book. Having failed in attracting his attention, Lalita pottered about with this and that, delayed without cause—but that too yielded no result, she had to leave perforce. But she could not leave now, without speaking to Shekhar. She was supposed to go to the theatre with some others in a short while; she stood and waited for Shekhar's permission to go.

Lalita did not take a single step without Shekhar's permission. No one had instructed her to do so, nor was there any reason for this. It was just that she had always taken his permission; that was how things had been, for a long time, and never had she ever questioned or argued with this unspoken rule even once in her mind. With the intelligence that comes naturally to any human being, Lalita was conscious of the fact that while others could do as they pleased, go where they wanted to, she could not. Lalita was not independent, and the permission of her uncle and aunt would not suffice either. From behind the door she gently said, 'Er, we are going to the theatre.'

Her mild tones did not reach Shekhar, so she received no reply from him.

Lalita then raised her voice slightly and said, 'They are all waiting for me!'

He must have heard her this time, for now Shekhar put aside his book and asked, 'What is the matter?'

Slightly aggrieved, Lalita responded, 'At last you hear

me! We are going to the theatre.'

Shekhar asked, 'Who is "we"?'

'Annakali, Charubala, Mama and I.'

'Who is this Mama?'

Lalita answered, 'His name is Girin Babu; he came here about five days back; he has come from Munger to study for his graduation from here—a fine person!'

'I see—you are already friends with him, are very familiar with his name and profession etc! Now I understand why there has been no sight or sound of you for the last four to five days. Busy playing cards I suppose?'

Lalita was a bit taken aback and scared at Shekhar's manner of speaking. She had not even thought that he could ask her such a question so she was at a loss for words.

Shekhar continued, 'You have been playing a lot of cards these days, isn't that true?'

Swallowing nervously, Lalita quietly answered, 'But Charu said....'

'Charu said? What did she say?' Suddenly noticing that she was quite dressed up, Shekhar said, 'I see that you have come all dressed—all right, go.'

But Lalita found it difficult to leave and stood there in silence.

Charubala was her next-door neighbour and best friend. Her family belonged to the Brahmo sect. Besides Girin, Shekhar knew them all. It was seven years since Girin had last visited their neighbourhood. He had been a student at Bankipur in the interim and there had been no need for him to come to Kolkata. Hence Shekhar was not acquainted with him. Observing Lalita still standing there he said, 'Why are you waiting here senselessly? You can leave,' and immediately held the book up to his face.

After standing silently for another five minutes or so, Lalita once again quietly asked, 'Shall I go?'

'I told you to, didn't I, Lalita?'

Observing Shekhar's mood, Lalita was no longer in any frame of mind to go to the theatre; but it was also going to be very difficult to cancel plans. It had been decided that she would bear half the expenses and that Charu's uncle would be responsible for the rest.

Lalita was well aware that everyone was waiting for her impatiently and that their impatience would surely increase in proportion to the time they were being forced to wait. She could visualize all this, yet could not think of what to do. It was out of the question to go without permission. Remaining silent for a couple of minutes, she said, 'Only this one time, Shekhar da, may I go?'

Putting the book aside, Shekhar said harshly, 'Lalita, if you want to, please go; you are old enough to decide what to do. Why ask me all this?'

Lalita was startled. It was nothing new to be scolded by Shekhar; in fact, she was used to it. But in the last two to three years she had heard nothing like this. Obviously, he was displeased with the idea of this outing. But her friends were still waiting for her and she too had come all dressed; it was only now, when she had come to get the money, that the problems had arisen. Now, what could she possibly tell them?

So far Lalita had never been forbidden by Shekhar to go anywhere. Having come to take his agreement almost for granted, she had got all dressed up today for a trip to the theatre. But now, not only was that liberty so abruptly curtailed, but the reason behind it was a cause of such shame that Lalita had never experienced in all her thirteen years; she felt it with every iota of her being. She stood there a few minutes more in hurt silence and then silently left, wiping eyes brimming over with tears. On reaching home, she sent for Annakali through a maid and handing her the money said, 'I am not well at all Kali, tell my friend that it is impossible for me to go with you.'

Annakali asked, 'What is the matter, Lalita di?'

'My head aches, I feel nauseous...very sick,' saying which Lalita turned over to face the wall. Charu then turned up and tried unsuccessfully to persuade her by whatever means; she even got her aunt to put in a word, but to no avail at all. The ten rupees in her hand made Annakali thoroughly restless and raring to go. Afraid that the programme itself would be cancelled in all this furore, she called Charu aside and showing her the money said, 'If Lalita di is all that ill, she might as well not go, Charu di! She has given me the money; let us all go.' It was apparent to Charu that despite being the youngest, Annakali was by no means lacking in intelligence. She agreed soon enough and all of them left together——without Lalita.

3

CHARUBALA'S MOTHER, MANORAMA, LIKED NOTHING BETTER than to play cards. But, she was not as good at the game as she was obsessed with it. This handicap was rectified when Lalita was present as her partner, since the latter was an extremely adroit player. Ever since the arrival of Manorama's cousin Girin, there had been marathon card sessions in Manorama's room throughout the afternoon. Girin played well so Lalita was an absolute necessity if Manorama wanted to match her cousin evenly.

The day after the trip to the theatre, finding her absent at the scheduled time for the card session, Manorama sent the maid-servant over to Lalita's house. Lalita was translating from an English text into Bengali and refused to leave her books.

When Lalita's friend also failed in persuading her, Manorama herself came over. Casting aside Lalita's books, she said, 'You need not break your back over these books Lalita, for you will be no magistrate once you grow up; rather, play a good game of cards. Come along!'

Lalita felt herself hemmed in; tearfully she reiterated that it was impossible for her to go that day, she would surely do so the next day. Manorama refused to listen to reason and informing Lalita's aunt, forcibly left with Lalita. Hence, that day too she had to sit opposite Girin and play cards. But the game was not much fun that day. Lalita just could not concentrate in any way; she remained tense all the while and as soon as dusk fell, she left. Girin took the opportunity to remark, 'You sent over the money yesterday, but did not accompany us; why don't we go again tomorrow?'

Shaking her head, Lalita mildly replied, 'No, I was very sick.'

Smiling, Girin said, 'You have recovered now, tomorrow is an absolute must.'

'No, no, tomorrow I will have no time,' Lalita made a rapid exit. It was not just Shekhar's anger that had distracted her that day, she herself had been overcome by an acute sense of embarrassment by what Shekhar had implied.

Like Shekhar's house, she was used to moving in and out of Charu's house too; she mixed with everyone comfortably as if she was a member of the household. Hence she had no compunction about meeting or talking to Charu's uncle Girin Babu. However, that day, throughout the entire card session, she could not help remembering Shekhar's remarks and think that in spite of knowing her for a very short period, Girin looked on her with more interest than was warranted. That a man's admiring glance could be so shameful, she had never imagined.

For just a while she stopped by at home, and then went directly to Shekhar's house and started work right away.

Since childhood she was the one to see to all the small chores of his room—clearing away the clutter of books, keeping the table neat and tidy and seeing to it that pens were clean and ink kept ready for use; no one else did all this—this was Lalita's prerogative and responsibility. She started the process of tidying up immediately, so as to be done before Shekhar returned.

Whenever she got the opportunity, she would hover about the house and because she looked on everyone as her own family, she too was treated as such by everybody. On losing her parents at the age of eight, Lalita had become a part of her uncle's household; since then, like a younger sibling, she had moved in an orbit around Shekhar and progressed in her studies under his tutelage.

All were aware that she held a very special place in Shekhar's affections, but none knew the depths to which that affection had reached, least of all Lalita herself. Since childhood everyone had seen Shekhar showering her with so much fondness that nothing seemed out of place or unseemly. Perhaps because it did not, neither did the possibility that she might one day take her place as a young bride of the household ever dawn on anyone. No one in Lalita's family had thought about it, nor had the thought ever occurred to Bhuvaneshwari.

Lalita had planned on completing her chores and leaving before Shekhar appeared; however, she was so involved in tidying up his room that she lost track of time. Suddenly the sound of footsteps alerted her and she immediately stood aside.

As soon as he saw her Shekhar remarked, 'There you are! So, how late did you return yesterday?'

Lalita did not answer.

Leaning back comfortably in an armchair, Shekhar continued, 'At what hour did you come back? Two? Three? Why aren't you replying?'

Lalita remained silent.

Irritated, Shekhar dismissed her, 'Go downstairs, Mother wants you.'

Bhuvaneshwari was organizing a light meal. Lalita went up to her and asked, 'Ma, did you want me?'

'No, why?' Looking up at Lalita she asked, 'Why are you looking so wan and washed out? Haven't you eaten as yet?'

Lalita shook her head.

Bhuvaneshwari said, 'All right, you carry this upstairs to your Dada and come back down to me.'

A little later, Lalita went upstairs with Shekhar's meal and observed that he was still sitting in that armchair with his eyes closed—he had not changed out of his office clothes, neither had he washed up. Coming close, she said softly, 'I have brought your food.'

Shekhar did not even look up at her. He simply said, 'Keep it somewhere and leave.'

Instead of doing so, Lalita continued to stand there, holding the tray in silence.

Even without opening his eyes Shekhar was aware that

Lalita had not left and was still standing there; after remaining silent for a couple of minutes he said, 'How long will you keep standing? I will take some time. Just put it down and go.'

Standing quietly, Lalita was steadily getting irked. In soft tones she said, 'It does not matter if it is late, I don't have any work downstairs.'

Looking up at her Shekhar smiled and said, 'Some words at long last! There might be no work below, but surely in the other house? Even if there is nothing in your house, there must be some work for you in some neighbour's house? After all, you do not have just one household to think about, do you, Lalita.'

'Definitely not!' she retorted, and banging down the tray in anger stormed out of the room.

Shekhar called after her, 'Come and see me in the evening.'

'I cannot keep moving upstairs and downstairs,' she muttered and left.

When she reached Bhuvaneshwari's room, she was told, 'You took your Dada's meal up, but what about the paan?'

'I am very hungry, Ma; I just cannot do any more. Let someone else take it up, please?' And Lalita sat down emphatically.

Looking at her agitated face, Bhuvaneshwari smiled a bit and said, 'You sit down and have your meal then, I'll send the maid up.'

Without another word, Lalita obeyed.

She had not gone to the theatre the day before, yet Shekhar had scolded her. Piqued, she didn't show her face to Shekhar for five days, but went to his room in the afternoons—when he was away at the office—and did all the chores. Shekhar, realizing his mistake, sent for her a couple of times, but she still did not turn up.

4

ONE MORNING, A FEW DAYS LATER, LALITA WAS IN A quandary. There was a certain beggar who used to frequent the locality periodically, and whenever he materialized, he would call out to Lalita, addressing her as Mother. According to the man, Lalita had been his mother in a previous birth and no sooner had he seen her than he had recognized her. Lalita had a great fondness for him and would always give him a rupee. The impossible blessings that he would shower on her, promising her the most improbable good fortunes, would thrill her no end. The beggar appeared that morning and called out in loud tones, 'O Mother, where are you?'

His call embarrassed Lalita somewhat. Shekhar was having a conversation with her uncle just then, so how could she venture into the room to fetch money? Looking this way and that, she finally approached her aunt. Having just emerged from a verbal battle with the maid, Lalita's aunt had grimly begun cooking; Lalita decided that it would be unwise to approach her at such a moment, and peeped out, only to find the mendicant firmly ensconced by the door. Never having sent him away empty-handed, she just could not bring herself to set a new precedent.

The man called out once again.

Annakali came running up and said, 'Lalita di, that "son" of yours is here.'

Lalita said, 'Kali, run an errand for me, please. I don't have a minute to spare right now. Please run to your Shekhar da and ask him for a rupee.'

Annakali ran off and in a little while came running back and handing Lalita a coin said, 'Here you are.'

Lalita asked, 'What did Shekhar da say?'

'Nothing! He told me to take the money from his coat pocket, which I did.'

'He didn't say anything else?'

'No, nothing,' said Annakali shaking her head, and left to play.

Lalita performed her charitable deed, but did not wait to listen to all the effusive blessings the beggar had in store for her; she just did not feel like it today.

The afternoon sessions of card-playing had been continuing full spate the past couple of days; but that afternoon Lalita excused herself on pretext of a headache. It was not entirely false though; she truly felt melancholic. In the evening, sending for Annakali she asked, 'Don't you go to Shekhar da these days to get your lessons explained?'

Annakali nodded, 'Why, yes!'

'Doesn't Shekhar da enquire about me?'

'No! Oh, yes, yes, he did so the day before yesterday— whether or not you played cards in the afternoon.'

Anxiously Lalita enquired, 'What was your answer?'

Annakali replied, 'I said that you played cards at Charu didi's house in the afternoon. Shekhar da then asked, "Who are the other players?" I told him that Manorama aunty, Charu didi, her uncle Girin Babu and you were the players. Tell me, Lalita di, who is a better player—you or Charu didi's uncle? Aunty always insists that you are the best; is that true?'

But Lalita was highly irritated. Not responding to Annakali's question, she snapped, 'Why did you have to talk so much? You must meddle in everything. In future I will never ever give you anything!' She left in a huff.

Annakali was amazed. She just could not grasp the reason for Lalita's sudden change of mood.

Manorama's card sessions ground to a halt over the next two days. From the very beginning Manorama had suspected that Girin had become greatly attracted to Lalita and in Lalita's absence her suspicions were now confirmed.

These past two days Girin had been somewhat restless and absentminded. In the evenings he would not go out for a stroll as was his normal routine; all of a sudden he would enter the house and wander about purposelessly from room to room. He turned up that afternoon and said, 'Didi, today too there will be no game?'

Manorama answered, 'How is it possible, Girin? Where are the participants? Oh well, we three might as well play together…'

Somewhat unenthusiastically Girin responded, 'Is a game possible with three people, Didi? Why don't you send for Lalita?'

'She will not come.'

Mournfully Girin asked, 'Why won't she? They have forbidden her to come, I suppose?'

Manorama shook her head, 'No, her uncle and aunt are not people of that ilk. It is her own choice not to turn up!'

In sudden cheer Girin spoke up, 'Then, surely if you go one more time personally, she definitely will!' Then, suddenly conscious of his eagerness for Lalita's company, he immediately felt embarrassed.

Manorama laughed, 'Fine, then that is what I will do!' She left and returning with Lalita some time later sat down for a game of cards.

Because there had been no play for two days, the session warmed up very soon. Lalita and her partner were winning.

About an hour or two later Annakali appeared all of a sudden and beckoned Lalita, 'Lalita di, Shekhar da is calling, hurry up!'

Lalita's face paled; she stopped dealing out the cards and asked, 'Hasn't Shekhar da left for office?'

'I don't know. Maybe he has returned,' said Annakali and left.

Lalita put aside the cards and looking apologetically at Manorama said, 'I must go.'

Grasping her hands Manorama said, 'What's that! Why don't you continue for a couple more games?'

In a flurry, Lalita merely said, 'That's impossible—it will really anger him,' and rushed off.

Girin asked, 'Who is this Shekhar da, Didi?'

Manorama answered, 'He lives in that large house with the gates—that house which stands at the head of the street.'

Nodding, Girin responded, 'Oh, that house! So Nabin Babu is their relative?'

Manorama exchanged glances with her daughter and smiled, 'Some relative! That wily old man is just waiting for a chance to usurp even the little land that Lalita's family owns.' Girin looked on in astonishment.

Manorama then told him how the previous year, Gurucharan's second daughter's marriage had been stuck because of financial constraints, and how Nabin Roy had lent him the money at an appalling high rate of interest, and in lieu got the house mortgaged to him. It would be impossible for Lalita's uncle to ever repay the money and ultimately Nabin Roy would possess the house.

After revealing all the facts, Manorama opined that the old man craved to completely raze to the ground Gurucharan's dilapidated house and build a grand house for the younger son, Shekhar; one house each for a son, not a bad idea at all.

An overwhelming sense of distaste overcame Girin. He asked, 'But Didi, Gurucharan Babu also has other daughters, how will he marry them off?'

Manorama could only answer, 'Not just his own, there is Lalita too. She has no parents, the entire responsibility of her marriage too lies with that poor man. She is growing up fast and will somehow have to be married off this year. In their Brahmin society there is none to help them—all have a fixation about caste. We Brahmos are much better off, Girin.'

Girin had nothing to say and she continued, 'The other day, her aunt started weeping in my presence as she spoke about Lalita. She didn't have any idea of what could be arranged or how. Just worrying about her, Gurucharan Babu can barely bring himself to eat. Girin, isn't there anybody amongst your group of friends in Munger, whose only consideration in a marriage will be the girl? It truly is very difficult to find a gem of a girl like Lalita.'

Dismally and with the bare vestiges of a smile Girin responded, 'Where will I garner friends from, Didi? But I can help out with money.'

As a doctor, Girin's father had amassed a lot of money and property——and Girin was the sole inheritor.

Manorama asked, 'You will lend them money?'

'Would it be lending? If he so desires Gurcharan Babu can return the sum; if not, that is fine too.'

This amazed Manorama. 'But Girin . . . what do you stand to gain by giving them so much money? Neither are they our relatives, nor do they belong to the same caste. Who is charitable these days without reason?'

Girin looked at his sister and then, laughing, said, 'They may not be from the same social strata, but they are Bengalis, aren't they? He is in dire need and I have plenty—why don't you broach the subject, Didi? If he is willing to accept,

I am ready to give the money. Lalita is nobody of theirs and nobody of ours either; what does it matter if I bear the entire expenses of her wedding?'

Manorama was not particularly pleased with his reply. True, she did not stand to gain or lose in any way by this transaction; but the idea of one person giving another large sums of money without asking for anything in return displeases many a female deeply.

Charu who was quietly listening to the conversation now piped up, absolutely thrilled, 'Please do that Mama, let me go and give Lalita's aunt the news.'

She immediately received a chiding from her mother for her interference, 'Stop it, Charu! Children should have no part to play in such conversations! If anything is to be said, I will do the needful.'

Girin responded, 'You do that, Didi. The day before yesterday I met Gurucharan Babu by the roadside and talked for a very short while with him. He seems to be quite a simple man, what do you say?'

Manorama replied, 'I quite agree. Husband and wife, both are simple people. That is what is so sad, Girin—a man like that might be rendered homeless and shelterless. Haven't you witnessed that for yourself, Girin—didn't you see the way Lalita ran when Shekhar Babu called? It is as though the entire household is in bondage to them. But, no matter what services are rendered, once in the clutches of Nabin Roy, there is not much hope of being rescued from that plight.'

Girin asked, 'Then, will you broach the subject, Didi?'

'All right, I will. If you can help by being charitable, so be it.' Smiling a bit, Manorama questioned, 'Anyway, why are you so concerned, Girin?'

'What other interest could I have, Didi? It's an act of kindness to help out someone in distress,' and Girin departed in a somewhat embarrassed manner. No sooner had he left, than he returned once again.

His sister enquired, 'Now what?'

With a smile Girin commented, 'All these tales of woe—perhaps everything is not true.'

Surprised, Manorama asked, 'Why do you say that?'

Girin explained, 'The manner in which Lalita spends money is not at all like one poverty stricken. The other day we had gone to the theatre. Lalita did not accompany us, but sent ten rupees through her sister. Why don't you ask Charu about the manner in which she spends freely; her personal expenses are nothing less than twenty-five rupees a month.'

Manorama found it impossible to believe all this.

Charu said, 'True, Ma; but all that is Shekhar Babu's money. It is not just now that this is happening—ever since her childhood she has always opened Shekhar da's almirah and taken money, nobody says anything.'

Looking at her daughter Manorama asked suspiciously, 'Does Shekhar Babu know about her taking money?'

Charu nodded vigorously, 'Yes, she opens the drawer and takes money in his very presence. Last month, who do you think gave so much money at Annakali's doll's wedding? It was Lalita who bore all the expenses!'

Pondering on the matter Manorama could only say, 'I really do not know what to think. But it is certainly true that the boys are not tight-fisted like their father; they have taken after their mother and have a kind disposition and are religious minded too. Besides, Lalita is supposed to be an extremely nice girl. She has been brought up in close proximity to them throughout her childhood; she looks on Shekhar almost as her own brother—probably that is why they are all so fond of her. Charu, you are always in touch with them. Isn't Shekhar supposed to be getting married this winter? I believe the old man will collect a huge amount of dowry!'

Charu responded, 'Yes Ma, this winter—everything has been settled, I heard.'

5

GURUCHARAN BABU WAS THE KIND OF PERSON WHOM people of all ages found it easy to get along with. On a mere two-to-three days' acquaintance, an easy friendship had sprung up between him and Girin. Gurucharan loved to argue, though he had no firm convictions of his own, and in the same manner, he in no way took umbrage at being vanquished in battle either.

He would invite Girin over for a cup of tea in the evening. The day would be all but over by the time Gurucharan got back from office. While washing up he would ask, 'Lalita, can I have a cup of tea, dear? Kali, go on and ask your Girin Mama to drop by.' Then, endless arguments would begin over innumerable cups of tea.

Sometimes Lalita would sit quietly by her uncle and listen to the conversation. On those days Girin would virtually spew forth arguments and counter-arguments. Quite often the debate would be against the ills of modern society. The heartlessness of society, illogical persecution and torture—all these were aspects that were heatedly discussed by the two men.

Though there was virtually nothing concrete to support their statements, Girin's thoughts found an echo

in Gurucharan's turbulent and worry-ridden heart.
Ultimately he would nod and say, 'You are right, Girin. Who
does not want to see his daughter married well at the right
time? But then, how does one do so? According to the
dictums of society, if a girl has grown up, get her married.
But, do they help with the arrangements? Take my example,
Girin, this very house has been mortgaged in the process
of arranging for a daughter's wedding. In a short while I
will have to take to the streets with my family. Society will
then not say, "Come, take shelter in my house." What do
you say?'

If Girin wanted to reply to this question, he wouldn't
be given a chance, for Gurucharan would provide all the
replies himself. 'Very true!' he would say. 'It is best that
caste disappears from society. Then, whether we eat or not,
at least we can live in peace. A society that does not
sympathize with the poor, does not help in moments of
crisis and can only threaten and punish—such a society is
not for me, or for those who are poor like me; it is a society
for the rich. Fine, let the rich remain, there is nothing in
such a society for us.' And, having spoken his mind out so
boldly, Gurucharan would fall silent.

Lalita did not merely listen with rapt attention to all
the arguments, but at night would try to logically
understand all that had been said, thinking them over till
she fell asleep. Lalita loved her uncle, so whatever Girin
said in support of her uncle's viewpoint seemed to be the
veritable truth to her. Her uncle was becoming so agitated

primarily because of her; he was almost forgetting to eat or drink—so overburdened was he; her peace-loving Mama, he was in such turmoil only because he had taken her under his wing! If he did not get her married off soon, he would become a social outcast, for harbouring an overage unmarried woman. But if I marry and return home a widow, Lalita thought, then there will be no shame. But, where is the difference between a widow and a spinster! Why should giving shelter to one be shameful, while giving shelter to the other was perfectly acceptable?

The daily conversations that she heard were obviously leaving a deep impression on Lalita's mind. An echo of Girin Babu's comments would emerge when she was alone, and once again, thoroughly analysing them, Lalita would think to herself, 'Truly, all that Girin Babu says is extremely logical,' and fall asleep.

Lalita could not but have a high opinion of or be in absolute compliance with anyone who tried to understand her uncle's problems and reach out to him. At present that person was Girin and she began to worship him in earnest.

Gradually she too, like Gurucharan, began to look forward to the tea sessions in the evening.

Initially Girin used to address Lalita rather formally. But Gurucharan forbade him to do so, and requested him to treat her normally. Ever since, Girin had progressed to a casual intimacy.

One day Girin asked, 'Don't you have tea, Lalita?'

Lowering her eyes, Lalita shook her head; Gurucharan

replied, 'Her Shekhar da has forbidden it. He does not like women drinking tea.'

It was clear to Lalita that the reply did not please Girin.

On Saturdays, the tea session used to go on till much later than usual and it was a Saturday that day. They had finished with drinking tea; Gurucharan had not been able to participate all that wholeheartedly in the discussions that had been initiated by Girin today—every once in a while he would lose his concentration and become absentminded.

Girin noticed this and asked, 'Perhaps you are not feeling very well today?'

Removing the hookah from his mouth, Gurucharan responded, 'I am absolutely fine.'

Hesitantly and somewhat awkwardly Girin prodded gently, 'Then perhaps something at the office...'

'No, it's not even that,' Gurucharan looked at Girin with a certain degree of surprise. He was such a simple soul that he had no idea at all that his inner turmoil was leaving an external imprint in his manner.

Earlier Lalita might not have intervened, but she had recently begun participating in the discussions once in a while. She said, 'Yes, Mama, today you are seeming out of sorts.'

Gurucharan laughed aloud, 'Oh, it's like that, is it? Yes, you are right, I am not in a very positive frame of mind.'

Both Girin and Lalita gazed at him.

Gurucharan continued, 'In spite of being aware of my

circumstances, Nabin da chose to be extremely insulting towards me today, that too, in full public view. But, one cannot really blame him either—it's been over six months and I have not been able to pay back even a bit of the interest, let alone the capital.'

Knowing the delicacy of the issue, and gauging the true extent to which her uncle was overcome by helplessness, Lalita became extremely anxious to change the subject at any cost. In fear that her uncle would wash all the dirty family linen in front of an outsider, she quickly said, 'Don't worry Mama, all that can come later.'

But Gurucharan did not say anything explicitly as Lalita has feared. Rather, he smiled wanly and said, 'What can happen later, dear? You see, Girin, this daughter of mine is like a mother to me—she does not want her aged son to worry about anything at all. The difficulty, Lalita, is that outsiders do not even want to acknowledge that your poor Mama has any problems!'

Girin asked, 'What did Nabin Babu have to say, today?'

Lalita, being unaware that Girin already knew all the facts, steadily grew more and more angry at this unwarranted curiosity of the guest.

Gurucharan revealed all. Apparently Nabin Roy's wife had been plagued by a stomach ailment for a very long time. Recently it had begun to act up to such a degree that the doctors had advised a complete change of environment. Money was needed and so Nabin Babu had demanded payment of all the interest that was due to him, as well as some of the capital.

Girin remained silent for a while. And then mildly remarked, 'There is something that I have been meaning to say, but felt hesitant; if you do not object, allow me to do so today.'

Gurucharan laughed aloud, 'Nobody ever hesitates about telling me anything. What is it, Girin?'

Girin answered slowly, 'Didi tells me that Nabin Babu charges very high rates of interest. There is a lot of my money just lying fallow—why not use it to pay off the debt?'

Both Gurucharan and Lalita were astounded. Girin continued awkwardly, 'At the moment I do not have much use for money; if it can come of use to you I suggest you take it now and return it at any point of time in the future which is convenient to you. I am all right with it...'

Gurucharan asked slowly, 'You will pay the entire sum of money?'

Girin very diffidently said, 'Yes, if that will ease you of some of your burdens...'

Gurucharan was about to make some sort of response, when Annakali came rushing in, 'Lalita di, hurry, Shekhar da had told us to get ready; we will all be going to the theatre.' She then rushed out in the same manner that she had entered. Her fervent enthusiasm made Gurucharan laugh. Lalita stood unmoving.

Annakali returned in a flash, impatiently asked, 'You haven't yet gone in, Lalita di? We are all waiting!'

In spite of the renewed appeal Lalita showed no signs of movement. She wanted to know her uncle's final decision; but Gurucharan looking at Annakali smiled and said to Lalita tenderly, 'Go on then, dear, don't delay——they are all waiting for you.'

Lalita thus had no option but to leave. As she turned to leave she cast a look of deep gratitude at Girin, which the latter had no difficulty in perceiving.

About ten minutes later, after having got ready, Lalita silently entered the room once again on the pretext of handing out some mouth fresheners.

Girin had left. Gurucharan lay with a thick pillow supporting his head and tears running down his face. It was apparent to Lalita that these were tears of joy. Hence, she went out of the room just as she had silently tiptoed in.

A little later when she appeared in Shekhar's room, Lalita's eyes too were brimming over with tears. Annakali was not there; she had been the first to seat herself in the car. Shekhar had been waiting (probably for Lalita) all alone in his room; and looking up at her, he noticed her tear-filled eyes.

Not having seen Lalita for about ten days, he had grown steadily more and more irritable. But, presently, he forgot all that and greatly concerned, solicitously enquired, 'What is the matter, why are you crying?'

Lalita lowered her head, and shook it vigorously.

Having her out of sight for several days had brought about a distinct change in Shekhar; he suddenly drew closer and holding her by the shoulders, forced Lalita to look up, 'Why, you truly are weeping, what has happened?'

Lalita could no longer control herself, she sat down where she was and, burying her face in the end of her sari, began to sob copiously.

6

AFTER COUNTING OUT THE NOTES GIVEN TO HIM AS FULL payment for both capital and interest, Nabin Roy returned the mortgage papers and asked, 'So, who gave you the money?'

Gently, Gurucharan responded, 'Don't ask me that, it is a secret.'

Nabin Roy was not at all pleased at getting back the money—he had not wanted the loan to be repaid, nor was he expecting it. Rather, he had planned that by harassing Gurucharan and pressurizing him incessantly, he would manage to drive the poor man out of his mortgaged house. That would pave the way for Nabin Babu to demolish the present building and construct a massive house in its place. Making a barbed remark he said, 'But of course, now it is a secret! The fault is not yours, but mine. It was wrong of me to have asked for the money back, wasn't it? Look at the times on which we have fallen!'

Hurt, Gurucharan responded, 'What kind of talk is that, Dada? It is merely the money that you had lent that I have returned, I still remain indebted to you for your great kindness.'

Nabin Babu smiled. He was extremely worldly wise,

or else it would have been impossible for him to have amassed such wealth. He continued, 'If you had really believed that, you would not have rushed to repay me in this hurried and unseemly fashion. So what if I reminded you once about the money—and that too for my ailing wife, not for myself. But tell me, for how much have you mortgaged the entire house?'

Gurucharan shook his head and said, 'It has not been mortgaged and neither has there been any talk of interest.'

This was hard for Nabin Babu to believe, 'What, so much money just on trust?!'

'Yes indeed, something of the sort. The boy is very nice and extremely kind.'

'Boy? Who is this boy?'

Gurucharan fell silent. He should not have revealed even the little that he already had.

Gauging his trend of thought, Nabin Babu smiled and said, 'Since it is forbidden to reveal the name of your benefactor, let me not bother you any further. But I have seen a lot of the world and let me give you fair warning. This do-gooder—let him not cause you even greater distress in these attempts to provide succour.'

Without making any response to that remark, Gurucharan bade a polite farewell and left with the papers.

Every year at about this time, Bhuvaneshwari spent some time in the west. It helped in providing some relief to her ailing stomach, though her condition was nothing very grave. Nabin Babu had grossly exaggerated the state of affairs when he was speaking to Gurucharan the other day, in order to achieve his own ends. Be that as it may, arrangements were being made for the journey.

One morning, Shekhar was arranging his essentials in a suitcase. Annakali entered the room and asked, 'Shekhar da, you all will be leaving tomorrow, won't you?'

Looking up Shekhar said, 'Kali, just call your Lalita di— let her put in now whatever she wants to take.' Every year Lalita accompanied them, taking care of all Bhuvaneshwari's needs and comforts, so it was natural for Shekhar to presume that she would be travelling with them this time too.

Shaking her head, Annakali replied, 'This year Lalita di will not be able to go.'

'Why not?'

Annakali answered, 'How can she? She will be getting married this winter. Baba is in search for a groom for her.'

Shekhar stared into space unblinkingly in silence.

Annakali, in all her enthusiasm, was blissfully unaware of his reaction and now came forward to whisper to him all that she had heard being discussed in the house, 'Girin Babu has said, no matter how much money is needed, a good groom must be found for Lalita di. Baba will not be going to the office today—he is visiting some boy somewhere for Lalita di; Girin Babu will be accompanying him.'

Shekhar heard all that was being said in silence and reasoned to himself that this was why Lalita had been reluctant to appear before him in the past few days.

Annakali continued, 'Isn't Girin Babu a very good man, Shekhar da? At the time of Mejdi's marriage, our house was mortgaged to Uncle; Baba was sure that within two to three months we would have no other option other than begging on the streets. So, Girin Babu provided the money. Yesterday Baba was able to return all the money to Uncle. Lalita di has said that we need not be scared any longer— that's true, isn't it, Shekhar da?'

Shekhar could not say a word in response but continued to stare unseeingly into space.

Annakali asked, 'What are you thinking about, Shekhar da?'

Coming back to his senses, Shekhar swiftly answered, 'No, nothing at all. Kali, quickly go and call your Lalita di—say that I want her; run and fetch her.'

Annakali ran off to convey the message.

Shekhar sat there staring fixedly at the open suitcase. All that he needed, all his requirements—they all seemed to have become redundant to him.

On hearing that she had been called, Lalita came upstairs; but before coming in she peeped through the window. Shekhar was sitting very still and staring fixedly at a point on the floor. She had never seen him look like this before. Lalita was a bit taken aback and somewhat scared. No sooner had she silently entered than Shekhar beckoned to her and stood up quickly.

Softly Lalita asked, 'Did you send for me?'

'Yes.' Shekhar remained still for a while and then said, 'I am leaving with Mother by the morning train tomorrow. It might be a while before we are back. Take the keys; the money for your expenses is in the drawer.'

Looking at the open suitcase, Lalita couldn't help remembering the joyous anticipation with which she had packed the previous time, and now, her Shekhar da was doing all the packing himself.

Both of them fell silent. Lalita realized that Shekhar had come to know that this time she would not be accompanying them. Perhaps he also knew of the reason; as she thought of this, Lalita seemed to shrink into herself in embarrassment. Turning away from her, Shekhar coughed once and clearing his throat said, 'Take care, if you are in particular need of anything, get my address from Dada and write me a letter.' Then suddenly he said, 'All right, you can leave now, I have to get all this organized. It is getting late and I will also have to stop by at the office.'

Lalita knelt down before the suitcase and said, 'Go and have your bath Shekhar da, I will complete the packing.'

'That will be perfect,' and leaving the keys with Lalita, Shekhar was about to leave the room, when he came to an abrupt halt. 'You haven't forgotten what all has to be packed for me, have you?'

Lalita began to examine the contents of the suitcase carefully and did not say a word.

Shekhar went downstairs and confirmed from his mother that all that Annakali had said was true. It was a fact that Gurucharan had repaid his debt. And a groom was indeed being sought in earnest for Lalita. Shekhar did not feel like asking any more questions; he retired for his bath.

After about an hour or two, on completion of his bath and meal, when Shekhar re-entered his room, he was amazed.

These two hours or so Lalita had done nothing at all; leaning against the lid of the open suitcase, she had simply sat there in silence. Startled into awareness at the sound of Shekhar's footsteps, she looked up and almost immediately lowered her eyes again. Her eyes were bloodshot.

But Shekhar appeared to notice nothing; changing into his formal clothes, he said easily, 'You will not be able to do it now, complete the packing in the afternoon.' He left for office. The reason for Lalita's turmoil was clear to him, but without giving careful thought to all possibilities, he did not want to broach the subject with her or with anyone else.

That evening in her house Lalita was all but overcome with waves of embarrassment when she brought in the tea. Shekhar was seated there along with Girin. He had come to take leave of Gurucharan.

Head bent, Lalita poured two cups of tea and placed them in front of Girin and her uncle. Immediately Girin spoke up, 'Where is the tea for Shekhar Babu, Lalita?'

Not looking up, Lalita responded softly, 'Shekhar da

does not have tea.'

Girin did not comment any further, he remembered what he had heard. Shekhar did not have tea, and he did not approve of others having it either.

Picking up his cup, Gurucharan broached the subject of the groom Girin and he had been to see for Lalita. The boy was studying for his graduation; after volubly praising him, Gurucharan said, 'But, in spite of all this, our Girin did not like him. Of course, the boy is not good-looking, but what difference do looks make to a man? It suffices that he is qualified.' Gurucharan was keen to get Lalita married off by some means or the other—it would relieve him of a huge responsibilty.

Looking towards him with a smile Shekhar asked, 'Why did Girin Babu not like him? The boy is educated, is financially stable—all in all, a good groom.'

Shekhar had simply asked for the sake of asking, though in his heart of hearts he knew why the groom had not pleased Girin; he also knew that no groom, in fact, would ever be considered suitable as far as Girin was concerned! However, caught unawares, Girin could not come up with a ready answer and became flushed with embarrassment. Noticing this as well, Shekhar stood up and said, 'Kaka, tomorrow I leave with my mother—don't forget to intimate us at the right time.'

Gurucharan answered, 'How is that possible! You are all I have. Besides, nothing can be done without your mother's presence. After all, she is mother to Lalita as well. What do you say, Lalita?' Smiling, he turned around and asked, 'Eh, when did she leave?'

Shekhar said, 'She escaped as soon as the topic was broached.'

Gurucharan said, 'She is bound to do that; after all, Lalita is becoming worldly-wise now.' A deep sigh escaped him and he continued, 'My little one is a perfect blend of homeliness and intelligence. Such a bride is hard to come by, Shekharnath.' As he spoke the words, such a sweet shadow of deep-rooted affection was reflected on his gaunt and careworn face that both Girin and Shekhar could not but help but salute this elderly man in silence.

7

ESCAPING UNOBTRUSIVELY FROM THE TEA SESSION, LALITA
went straight to Shekhar's room and, pulling up his suitcase
below the powerful gas lights, was engrossed in folding
and neatly putting by Shekhar's woollens, when she saw
Shekhar enter the room. She looked up and turned
speechless in fright and amazement.

Just as a man who has lost all in a legal battle, emerges
from the court broken and defeated and seems to have no
connection with the hopeful, positive person that he was
before the verdict—Shekhar too seemed to have turned
into a virtual stranger for Lalita. The stamp of one who had
been rendered bereft of all was etched on his face. In
parched tones he asked, 'What are you doing, Lalita?'

Not answering, Lalita came closer, grasped his hands
and asked tearfully, 'What is the matter, Shekhar da?'

'Why, nothing at all,' Shekhar forced a smile. At Lalita's
touch he seemed to revive a bit. Sitting down on the nearby
couch, he repeated his question, 'What are you doing?'

Lalita answered, 'I have come to put in this thick
overcoat I had forgotten.' Shekhar looked at her in silence;
Lalita continued, a little more calmly, 'Last time the train
journey was very uncomfortable for you; there were a lot

of large coats, but none that were thick; so, immediately after our return, I had one tailored to your measurements.' Lalita picked up a very thick overcoat and brought it over to Shekhar.

Carefully examining it, Shekhar said, 'But, you didn't let me know a thing. Why?'

Lalita laughed, 'You all are fashionable gentlemen— would you have permitted me to make such a thick coat? So, instead of telling you, I had it tailored and stored.' Putting it away in the suitcase, she said, 'It's right on top, you'll find it as soon as you open the suitcase—don't forget to put it on if you are cold.'

'All right,' muttered Shekhar, staring ahead unblinkingly. Suddenly he spoke aloud, 'No, this is impossible, it just cannot happen.'

'What cannot happen? You will not wear it?'

Hastily he answered, 'No, no, that's not it, of course I will wear it. This is another matter altogether. Tell me, Lalita, do you know if everything else has been packed?'

Lalita answered, 'Yes, it is; I organized everything in the afternoon.' And, after re-examining all the articles, Lalita locked the suitcase.

Remaining silent for a while and looking in her direction, Shekhar asked sombrely, 'Can you tell me, Lalita, what my plight will be next year?'

Looking up, Lalita asked, 'Why?'

'You know only too well why!' As soon as he uttered the words, he attempted to cover up the matter, so he smiled wryly and said, 'However, before leaving for the house of another, explain and show me where things are kept—or else, I will never be able to find anything when I need it.'

Angrily Lalita said aloud, 'Go on!'

Shekhar laughed at long last. '"Go on". I understand it is a matter of embarrassment for you to discuss your marriage with me, but tell me honestly, what will my condition be? I have the desire to live well all right, but no ability at all to put that into effect! These are not things that a servant can do either; henceforth, I will have to become like your uncle—make do with one change of clothes, somehow or the other!'

Casting the bunch of keys on the ground, Lalita ran out.

Shekhar called after her, 'Be sure to come tomorrow morning.'

She heard him call her name, but couldn't bear to be there any more, for shame. Rapidly she ran down the stairs.

In one corner of the roof of their house, she discovered Annakali sitting in the moonlight with a pile of marigold flowers before her. Approaching her Lalita asked, 'What are you doing sitting out in the cold, Kali?'

Without looking up Annakali answered, 'Weaving garlands for my daughter, Lalita di. Tonight is her wedding.'

'You did not tell me earlier?'

'Nothing had been fixed, Lalita di. But Baba looked up the almanac and found that except for tonight, there is no other date for the rest of the month. My daughter is growing up and I cannot keep her at home any longer; I have to get her married tonight somehow or the other. Lalita di, give me some money to arrange for a feast.'

Lalita laughed. 'Only when you need money do you remember me! Go and take some from under my pillow. But, Kali, can marigold garlands be used for a wedding?'

Annakali responded solemnly, 'Yes, when nothing else is available! I have married off so many daughters, Lalita di! I know everything.' She went off to organize the food.

Lalita sat there and started weaving garlands for Annakali's doll's wedding.

Returning after a while, Annakali said, 'Everyone has been invited, only Shekhar da remains. I had better go and tell him, or else he will be offended.'

To hear Annakali speak, one would think that she was not a young, unmarried girl, but the most seasoned of housewives instead—meticulous in the extreme in everything she did. After intimating Shekhar, she came down and said, 'He wanted a garland. Lalita di, won't you please go and hand it to him? I can then get on with making all the arrangements here. There is so much to do, and not much time left before the auspicious hour gets over.'

Shaking her head Lalita responded, 'Impossible for me, Kali, you go yourself.'

'All right, I will. Hand me the large one.'

About to hand it over, Lalita changed her mind suddenly and said, 'Never mind, I'll take it across.'

With studied gravity, Annakali answered, 'That would be the best, Lalita di, I am extremely busy and don't have a moment to spare.'

Her way of speaking and expression made Lalita laugh and she left with the garland. From the door she observed Shekhar intently composing a letter; opening the door she came and stood behind him but he still failed to notice her. After remaining silent for a while, with the sole purpose of startling him, she quickly slipped the garland around his neck and immediately hid behind the couch.

Initially startled, Shekhar called out, 'You, Kali!' The next moment, seeing Lalita, he turned extremely grave and exclaimed, 'What is this you have done, Lalita!'

She got up and looking somewhat fearfully at him responded, 'Why, what is the matter?'

Maintaining the same serious demeanour, Shekhar said, 'Why, don't you know? Go and ask Kali what it means when garlands are exchanged tonight at this auspicious hour!'

Lalita immediately understood and blushing crimson ran out of the room exclaiming, 'No, no, never!'

Shekhar called out, 'No, Lalita, do not leave. There is something particularly important I have to say.'

Lalita could hear Shekhar but could not even think of halting to listen further. It was impossible for her to stop anywhere; she ran straight to her room, and collapsing on the bed, lay there with eyes shut tight.

These five to six years she had grown up in close

proximity to Shekhar, but had never heard anything like this from him! Till now, the serious and solemn Shekhar had never joked with her and that too on such an embarrassing topic—she couldn't even imagine that such words could be spoken by him. Curling up in embarrassment, Lalita lay there for some twenty minutes and then sat up. She was innately scared of Shekhar; he had asked her to stay because of some particular work and he might get angry if she disobeyed him. She sat up and pondered whether she should go across or not. The maid-servant from the other house was heard calling out loudly, 'Lalita Didi, where are you? Chhoto Babu is asking for you.'

Lalita came out and softly answered, 'I am coming...'

Going upstairs and opening the door she found Shekhar still engrossed in his letter. Standing silently for a long while, ultimately she asked, 'Why did you want me?'

Continuing to write Shekhar answered, 'Come closer and I will tell you.'

'No, tell me from here.'

Smiling to himself, once again Shekhar reiterated, 'Look what you did on an impulse!'

Agitated, Lalita immediately responded, 'Again you are...'

Turning around Shekhar said, 'Is it my fault? You began it all...'

'I have done nothing, you return that garland now!'

Shekhar answered, 'That's why I have sent for you, Lalita.

Come closer and I will return the garland. You have left half the gesture half done, come closer and let me give it completion.'

Leaning against the door, Lalita was silent for a while and then said, 'I am seriously telling you, if you continue joking in this manner, I will never come in front of you again. Please return that to me.'

Shekhar picked up the garland and said, 'Come and take it.'

'Throw it to me from there.'

Shaking his head, Shekhar said yet again, 'You will not get it unless you come close.'

'Then I have no need for it,' said Lalita angrily and left.

Shekhar called out, 'But, half the ceremony remains undone!'

'Fine, let it be!' Truly taking umbrage now, Lalita would not return.

But she did not go downstairs either. Instead she went to the far end of the open terrace on the east and holding on to the railing, stood there staring straight ahead. By then the moon had risen in the sky and the pale winter moonlight was flooding the surroundings. The sky above was startlingly clear. Glancing once in the direction of Shekhar's room, Lalita looked upwards. Her eyes started smarting with tears of hurt, shame and embarrassment. She was no longer such a child as to remain oblivious of the nuances of what had happened. Then, why had Shekhar joked so cruelly with her in this manner? She was old enough to know just how lowly and insignificant she was. She was fully conscious of the fact that everybody was tender and caring with her only because she was an orphan. There was no one Lalita could truly call her own and in reality, nobody actually bore any responsibility for her. That was probably why Girin, having no sort of ties with her, could propose to rescue her as he had.

Closing her eyes, Lalita reflected on how much lower down the rung her uncle stood in society, compared to Shekhar's family. In addition, she herself was only a ward of her uncle's. As of this moment, serious discussions were on about finding a suitable bride for Shekhar from an affluent background; sooner or later such a marriage would take place. Lalita had also heard Shekhar's mother speculating about how much money Nabin Roy was expecting from this union.

Then why did Shekhar suddenly insult her in this manner! Lalita was lost in these thoughts as she stared blankly into space—when turning around suddenly she found Shekhar standing there, laughing quietly! The strand of marigold that she had garlanded Shekhar with miraculously adorned her own neck now. Her voice almost choked and distorted by tears, she said, 'Why did you do this?'

'Why had you done it?'

'I did not do a thing,' said Lalita, and attempting to tear away the garland from around her neck, looked up at Shekhar. She did not have the courage to say anything further, but tearfully muttered, 'Only because I have no one to call my own are you insulting me like this!'

Shekhar had been smiling all this while, but Lalita's words stunned him. These were not childish words! He answered, 'Wasn't it rather you insulting me?'

Wiping away her tears, a little timorously Lalita asked, 'How did I do that?'

Standing still for a while, Shekhar said easily, 'Now, if you think a bit, you will have the answer. You were flying too high these days, Lalita; before leaving on my journey, I have put an end to that.' He then fell silent.

Lalita no longer had anything to say and she remained standing with head bowed. In the glistening moonlight, neither of them seemed to find any words. Only the conch shells being repeatedly sounded at Annakali's daughter's wedding reverberated all around.

After waiting mutely for a while, Shekhar spoke, 'Don't remain in this chill any longer, go inside.'

'I will.' Lalita knelt at Shekhar's feet to offer her respectful salutations before she left. Then she enquired gently, 'Now, tell me, what am I to do?'

Shekhar smiled in response. He hesitated for a moment and then, extending both hands, brought her close and bending a little, touched his lips lightly to hers. 'After tonight you will not have to be told, you will know what to do, Lalita.'

A shiver of some unknown feeling ran through Lalita's entire body. Moving away, she asked, 'Did you react in this manner simply because I garlanded you?'

Smiling, Shekhar disagreed, 'No, I have been reflecting on this for a number of days, but could not come to any conclusion. Today I took this decisive step because I realized that it was impossible for me to live without you.'

Lalita answered, 'But your father will be very angry when he hears and Ma will be hurt. No, this is impossible, Shek—'

'True, Baba will be angry, but Ma will be happy. Doesn't matter, what was inevitable has happened—neither can you ignore it, nor can I. Go downstairs now and take Ma's blessings.'

8

ONE DAY, ABOUT THREE MONTHS LATER, A WAN-FACED
Gurucharan entered Nabin Roy's room and was about to
sit down on the mattress next to him, only to hear the
latter shout out, forbidding him to do so: 'No, no, not
there—take that stool. I cannot have a bath again at this
hour! You've forsaken your religion, haven't you?'

Gurucharan sat on a stool some distance away, with his
head bent low. Four days ago, after going through all the
rituals, he had converted to the Brahmo creed. This
morning, the news, embroidered ably with colourful
rumours, had reached the ears of Nabin Roy, a staunch and
diehard Hindu. Sparks seemed to emit from Nabin Roy's
eyes, but Gurucharan remained mild as ever and continued
to sit there silently. Ever since he had taken the plunge
without consulting anybody, there had been no end to the
tears and unpleasantness at home.

Nabin Roy blazed forth, 'Tell me, is it true or not?'

Gurucharan raised his tear-filled eyes and said, 'Yes, it
is.'

'Why did you take this step? Your salary is only sixty
rupees, you——!' A choleric outburst choked Nabin Roy's
voice.

Wiping his eyes and clearing his throat, Gurucharan said, 'I was not in my senses, Dada. I did not know if my problems would lead me to putting a noose around my neck or whether I should surrender to the Almighty—I did not know which way to go. Ultimately, instead of committing suicide, I decided to submit to divinity . . . and so converted.'

Gurucharan left, drying his tears.

Nabin Roy thundered aloud after him, 'What an excellent decision! You couldn't commit suicide but strangled your religion instead. Get out and never show your face to us again! Seek the company of the likes of you. Get your daughters married off in any bedeviled household!' He turned away his face.

In sheer anger, with his pride hurt, Nabin Roy felt like taking some sort of revenge on Gurucharan, but could not figure out what to do. The thought that Gurucharan had escaped completely from his clutches and that it was highly improbable that he could be trapped again in the near future agonized him not a little. Ultimately, not able to hit upon any other solution, he called some workmen and got them to build a massive barricade between the two adjoining houses, blocking the easy access through the terraces.

Meanwhile, still away from Kolkata, Bhuvaneshwari got word of Gurucharan's conversion from Shekhar and burst into tears. 'Shekhar, who could have possibly given him this idea?'

Shekhar had a very fair idea of who was behind the idea; however, without going into it, he said, 'But Ma, you would all have ostracized him from society soon in any case! How would he have got all those daughters married? As a Brahmo, at least he won't have to pay their dowries.'

Shaking her head, Bhuvaneshwari asserted, 'Nothing ever remains the same forever, Shekhar. If the question of dowries for daughters became a reason for giving up one's religion, many others would have to do the same. The Almighty looks after all those whom He has sent below.'

Shekhar remained silent. Wiping away her tears, Bhuvaneshwari continued, 'If I had brought my daughter Lalita along, I would have had to find some solution to this problem, and I would definitely have come up with something. I had no idea that Gurucharan did not allow her to come with us because he had this move in mind. It seemed to me that he was genuinely looking out for a suitable groom for her.'

Looking at his mother, Shekhar remarked somewhat awkwardly, 'That's all right, Ma, you can still do something about that on your return! After all, it is not Lalita who has converted to Brahmoism, it's merely her uncle. She isn't even part of his family, really; only because Lalita is an orphan is she being brought up there.'

Thinking it over, Bhuvaneshwari responded, 'Yes, true, but your father is not likely to agree to that. Perhaps he will not permit any sort of contact with them at all now.'

Shekhar himself was quite concerned about this point;

but he did not want to continue the conversation, and left the room.

He now felt not the slightest desire to remain away from Kolkata even a minute longer. After moving about restlessly, with an overcast and gloomy face, over the next couple of days, he finally went to his mother one evening and said, 'This is no longer enjoyable, Ma, let us return.'

Bhuvaneshwari immediately agreed, 'I too am not liking it here at all, Shekhar.'

On their return, mother and son found a boundary wall blocking the common passage between the two houses. It was obvious to both, even without a word being said, that the head of the Roy household had no intention of keeping even a nodding acquaintance, let alone form any sort of relationship, with Gurucharan's clan.

While Shekhar was having dinner that night, his mother said, 'They are talking of getting Lalita married to Girin. I had guessed as much beforehand.'

Without looking up, Shekhar asked, 'Who said so?'

'Her aunt! While your father was taking a nap in the afternoon, I went across to meet her. She has been weeping since Lalita's uncle converted and her eyes are now swollen and red.' Remaining silent for a while and wiping her own tears with the end of her sari, Bhuvaneshwari said, 'It is all fate, Shekhar, fate. No one can undo what fate has in store—whom can I blame? At least Girin is a good boy and well to do. Lalita will not suffer.'

Shekhar did not make any response but merely toyed

with the food on his plate. Soon after his mother left, he left his meal uneaten and after washing up, turned in for the night.

The next evening, he set out for a walk. At that time, the evening tea session was in full spate in Gurucharan's outer room—to the accompaniment of a lot of laughter and conversation. The sound of the clamour reaching his ears, Shekhar hesitated for a moment and then, entering the house, followed the sound and reached Gurucharan's room. Immediately the hubbub stopped and, looking at his face, the expressions of all present underwent a change.

Nobody there except Lalita was aware of the fact Shekhar had returned. That day, Girin and another gentleman were present; the stranger gazed in astonishment at Shekhar, while Girin stared gravely at the wall opposite. It was Gurucharan himself who had been speaking the loudest—and now his face turned absolutely ashen. Lalita sitting close by him was preparing the tea; she glanced up once and then lowered her head.

Shekhar moved closer and respectfully greeting Gurucharan, commented with a smile, 'Why, all the lights seem to have dimmed!'

Gurucharan probably blessed him in mild tones, but his voice could barely be heard. Shekhar could appreciate the other's dilemma at that moment and to give him some time, began to talk of himself. He mentioned returning by the previous morning's train, talked of his mother's recovery from her illness and described all the places they had visited. After talking breathlessly of all this and who knows what else, Shekhar ultimately glanced up at the face of the unknown youth.

Gurucharan had somewhat recovered his equilibrium by then, and introducing the young man said, 'He is our Girin's friend. They come from the same place, they have studied together—and he is a very good boy. Ever since we have been introduced, he drops in quite frequently to meet me, though he lives in Shyambazar.'

Nodding, Shekhar said to himself, 'A good boy, indeed!' Remaining silent for a while, he then asked, 'Kaka, is everything in order?'

Gurucharan did not reply; he sat with his head lowered. Seeing Shekhar get up to leave, he suddenly spoke up tearfully, 'Please do come by sometimes, don't desert us completely. You have heard all the news?'

'Most definitely I have,' saying which Shekhar moved towards the inner sanctum of the house.

Soon after, Gurucharan's wife's wails could be heard; sitting outside, Gurucharan wiped away his own tears with the end of his dhoti. Girin, with the demeanour of a culprit, gazed silently out of the window. Lalita had already left.

After a while, as he emerged from the kitchen and was about to step into the courtyard from the veranda, Shekhar noticed Lalita waiting behind the darkened doors. Respectfully touching his feet she moved very close; raising her face in silence, she waited for a while. Then, withdrawing, she asked quietly, 'Why did you not reply to my letter?'

'What letter? I did not get any! What had you written?'

Lalita answered, 'A lot, but it does not matter. You have heard everything. Now, tell me, what is it that you wish me to do?'

In tones of amazement Shekhar asked, 'What difference will my saying anything make?'

Looking up at him in trepidation, Lalita asked, 'Why do you say that?'

'But of course, Lalita, whom can I command?'

'Why, me, who else?'

'Why you, particularly? Even if I were to, why would you listen?' Shekhar sounded grave and a little sad.

Now Lalita was greatly perturbed; coming close once more, she tearfully asserted, 'Go on, this is not the time for you to tease me. I beg of you, tell me what will happen? I cannot sleep at night for worry and fright.'

'Fright of what?'

'Honestly! Isn't it scary? You were not here and neither was Ma. Look at the absurd things Mama sometimes does! Now, what if Ma refuses to accept me?'

Shekhar fell silent for a while and then said, 'Yes, true, Ma will not want to accept you. She has heard that your uncle has accepted a lot of money from another. Besides, now all of you are Brahmos and we are Hindus.'

At this moment Annakali called out from the kitchen, 'Lalita di, Ma wants you.'

Lalita responded out loud, 'Coming!' Then, lowering her voice, she reiterated, 'It doesn't matter what Mama's religion is; whatever you are, that's what I am. If Ma cannot discard you, she will not be able to reject me either. You are talking about borrowing money from Girin Babu? I will return all that. The money to pay off his debt will have to be accepted sooner or later.'

Shekhar asked, 'Where will you get all that money from?'

Looking up once at Shekhar and remaining silent for a while, Lalita said, 'Don't you know where a woman gets money from? That's where I will get it from too.'

So far, though Shekhar had been speaking in a restrained manner, a searing heat seemed to be cauterizing him internally; sardonically he said, 'But, your Mama seems to have sold you off!'

In the darkness Lalita could not see Shekhar's face, but could make out the change in his tone. Firmly she asserted, 'That's all a lie. There is no one like my Mama, don't mock him. You might not be aware of his difficulties and problems, but the whole world knows.' Then, swallowing hard and somewhat hesitantly she continued, 'Besides, he took the money after I was married—so he has no right to sell me off, and nor has he. Only you have that right. Of course, you are more than capable of selling me off to avoid paying the money—if you so wish!'

Not waiting for Shekhar's reply, Lalita left hastily.

9

THAT NIGHT SHEKHAR WANDERED ABOUT AIMLESSLY FOR A long time, and then, returning home, wondered how that chit of a girl, Lalita, had learned to backchat in such a manner! How could she argue with him in such a shameless fashion?

Today he had been greatly astonished and incensed by Lalita's behaviour. However, if he had paused for a moment to analyse the cause of his anger, he would have clearly understood that it was not directed against Lalita, but against his own self.

These past couple of months, while he was away from home and without Lalita's company, Shekhar had not seen beyond the balance sheets of imagined joys and sorrows, material gains and losses, that had occupied his mind. But now it had become clear to him what a vital role Lalita had always played in his life, the indispensable part she occupied in his future plans, how difficult it was to survive without her, how painful—Shekhar brooded relentlessly on all this as he lay stretched out on the bed. Perhaps because Lalita had grown up as part of his family since childhood, Shekhar had never thought of singling her out particularly from amongst his parents or brothers and sisters. But there always had been a nagging concern in his mind that perhaps he might not be able to marry Lalita. His parents would not, in all possibility, consent to this marriage, perhaps she would belong to another—his mind ran in continual circles around this anxiety. Hence, before leaving Kolkata, he had tried to stem the flood of his worries by garlanding Lalita at the auspicious hour.

The news of Gurucharan's converting to another religion had filled him with the greatest disquietude and an overwhelming fear of losing Lalita. He was familiar with this train of thought. But Lalita's plain words had abruptly put a halt to his line of thinking, and his thoughts now flowed in another direction completely. His worries now were not about winning her; instead he was concerned about whether he would be able to give her up, if the need arose.

The marriage proposal from Shyambazar had not materialized. Ultimately the family had backed off from the prospect of paying so much dowry and neither had Shekhar's mother really liked the girl. Hence, Shekhar had escaped his cause of concern for the time being; but Nabin Roy had not forgotten the prospect of getting ten to twenty thousand rupees as dowry, and he had certainly not given up efforts in that direction.

Shekhar couldn't decide upon the course of action he had to take! The fact that what had happened that night between them could have such repercussions, that Lalita should so unwaveringly be convinced that indeed her marriage had taken place and that in all sanctity there could be no going back, were things Shekhar had not foreseen. Though he himself had in the heat of the moment asserted, 'What was inevitable has happened—neither can you ignore it, nor can I,' at the time he had been in no position to give the matter any serious thought, as he was able to do now.

That night, a glowing moon had graced the sky, moonlight had flooded the surroundings, a garland had adorned his loved one and there had been the thrill of the first physical proximity to his beloved; there had been the intense intoxication of tasting the sweetness of his sweetheart's lips. Then, self interest and worldly practicalities had not intruded upon the moment; the image of a money-minded, avaricious father had not surfaced in his mind. Shekhar had assumed that it would not be a problem to convince his mother who was fond of Lalita. If only his brother would intervene and soften matters with his father, perhaps the entire issue could be resolved amicably. Besides, Gurucharan had not isolated himself then in this manner. But now all hopes of a union with Lalita seemed annihilated. The Almighty Himself seemed to have turned His face away.

Truly, there was not much that Shekhar could do. He was absolutely sure that there was no way of convincing his father; bringing his mother around was also an impossibility. There was no point in even giving utterance to the thought.

Sighing deeply, Shekhar said aloud in a stifled voice, 'What is to be done?' He knew Lalita only too well, having all but brought her up himself; what she once decided was sanctioned by religion, she would not go against under any circumstances. Lalita was certain that religion recognized her as Shekhar's wife; that was why she felt she had the right to unhesitatingly approach him so closely in the darkness and raise her face to his.

There was talk of her marriage to Girin, but it would be impossible for anybody to get her to consent. It was just not feasible that she remain silent! She would definitely reveal all. Shekhar's face became flushed. Truly! He had not only exchanged garlands, but pulling her close had even kissed her! She had not prevented him, because she felt that there was nothing wrong in this and he had a right to do what he did. Now, whom could Shekhar answer to for his actions?

It was a fact that he could not marry Lalita without his parents' consent. However, if the cause for her marriage to Girin not taking place were made public, how would he be able to handle all the gossip that would reverberate all around?

10

HAVING DECIDED THAT IT WOULD BE IMPOSSIBLE FOR HIM to marry Lalita, Shekhar gave up all dreams of her. He spent the first couple of days tense and dreading that she would suddenly appear, that she would reveal all, that he would have to answer all the questions that would then be raised. But, no one raised any questions. It was not apparent whether any revelations had been made, but no one visited his house from Gurucharan's. The open terrace in front of Shekhar's room commanded a full view of Gurucharan's terrace. For fear of a chance sighting, Shekhar stopped going to the terrace altogether. However, when a month went by without any confrontation, he breathed a sigh of relief and told himself, 'After all, any woman would naturally be embarrassed about making such revelations.' He had heard that women would rather die than talk of such matters. Shekhar came to believe in this and in his heart of hearts was deeply thankful to them for this weakness. But why did peace continue to elude him? Even when he was reassured about secrecy being maintained, why did his heart overflow with an indescribable pain? Why did the very essence of his being suffer tremors of hopeless panic and trepidation? He would despondently wonder at times if Lalita would ever say anything at all. Perhaps she would remain silent even when she was handed over to the care of another. Why did the very thought of her marriage being solemnized and her departing for her husband's house seem to infuriate him internally and at the same time sear him externally?

Previously, instead of going out in the evenings, Shekhar would pace about on the open terrace outside his room. He now resumed this routine. However, not for a day did he catch sight of anybody on the other roof. Only once he caught sight of Annakali, who had come there for something. No sooner had his eyes fallen on her than she looked down and before Shekhar could decide whether or not to call out, she had disappeared. It was then brought home to Shekhar forcibly that even that child Kali had understood the meaning of the blockade between the two terraces.

Another month went by.

In the course of conversation Bhuvaneshwari one day asked, 'Have you ever seen Lalita all this while?'

Shaking his head Shekhar asked, 'No, why?'

His mother answered, 'Finding her on the roof after almost two months, I called out—my daughter seems to have become a different person altogether; thin, wan and old beyond her years. So much gravity—one would never guess that the child is only fourteen years old!' Bhuvaneshwari's eyes filled with tears; wiping them dry she said, 'What she was clad in was soiled and darned; I asked, "Don't you have other clothes, dear?" She said she did, but I don't believe her. She has never worn clothes given by her uncle; I used to buy them for her and I haven't given her anything these past six to seven months.' Bhuvaneshwari could not continue any further, she wiped her eyes with the end of her sari; she truly loved Lalita as her own daughter.

Shekhar remained silent, staring in another direction.

After a long time, Bhuvaneshwari continued. 'Besides me, she cannot ask anybody for anything. If she is hungry at an odd hour, once again, she comes only to me. She would keep hovering around me and just looking at her I could understand what she wanted. That is the thought that keeps going around in my head, Shekhar; Lalita moves about dispiritedly all the time, nobody understands or even asks after her. She has only me to care for her physical comforts; she not only addresses me as Mother, but also truly looks on me as one.'

Shekhar did not have the gumption to look his mother in the eye. He continued gazing in the direction he was staring into and said, 'That's all right, Ma, why don't you just send for her and after finding out her needs, make sure she is taken care of?'

'Why would she accept anything from me now? Your father has blocked even the common passage. What face do I have to give anything at all? Gurucharan Babu, in the throes of sorrow, might have blundered badly. We as people close to him, could have organized a penance and helped him atone. But instead we isolated him and cast him off totally! This much more I will also say, it is because of your father that Lalita's Mama has been forced to give up his religion. Your father has been hounding him repeatedly for payments—any man can over-react in disgust. I would say that Gurucharan Babu has taken the right decision. That boy Girin has proved much closer to him than we are—I am telling you, Lalita will be happy if she marries him. The marriage is next month, I believe.'

Suddenly Shekhar turned around and asked, 'Oh, is the ceremony next month?'

'That's what I hear.'

Shekhar had no further questions.

Maintaining a silence for a while, his mother then said, 'I heard from Lalita that her Mama is not keeping too well either. How will he? As it is there is no peace in his heart, and added to that a continual spate of tears in the house. There is no calm there, even for a minute.' Shekhar listened in silence.

The lane in which they lived was so narrow that two cars couldn't pass each other. About ten days later, Shekhar was on his way back from work when his office car was brought to a halt by a car parked in front of Gurucharan's house. Shekhar got down and upon asking was told that the vehicle belonged to a doctor—a doctor had been summoned.

As his mother had told him of Gurucharan's ill health,

Shekhar made his way directly to Gurucharan's bedroom instead of returning home. What he had suspected turned out to be true. Gurucharan lay on the bed, seemingly lifeless; on one side of the bed sat Girin and Lalita, looking careworn; on the other side was the doctor, carrying out his examination.

Gurucharan uttered some muffled words of welcome. Lalita, pulling one end of the sari even closer, looked the other way.

The doctor belonged to the same locality and knew Shekhar. He completed his tests, arranged for the medicines and left the room, accompanied by Shekhar. As Girin followed them out and settled the dues, the doctor emphasized that the disease had not become virulent, and that a simple change of air would work wonders. Once the doctor left, both returned to Gurucharan's room.

Lalita gesturing to Girin began to have a hushed conversation with him in one corner of the room; Shekhar sat in front of Gurucharan, looking at him silently. Gurucharan now lay with his back towards the door and was unaware of Shekhar's sitting by his side.

After a while Shekhar got up and left. Even then, Girin and Lalita remained in intimate conversation; neither had anybody asked him to be seated, nor did anybody see him out. There was nobody to address even a solitary remark to him or ask him a single question.

It was them that Shekhar realized only too definitely that Lalita had been released from his onerous responsibility—that he could now breathe a sigh of relief! There need no longer be any fear—Lalita would not involve him in any imbroglio! As he changed into his casual clothes in his room, Shekhar reminded himself innumerable times that now it was Girin who was the true friend of the family, the hope of all and provider of Lalita's future shelter. Shekhar himself was nobody at this moment of crisis. Lalita had no longer felt the need of even some verbal assurances from him now.

Exclaiming aloud, 'Oof!' Shekhar collapsed onto a padded couch. Seeing him, Lalita had withdrawn in a pointed manner that made it only too clear that he was a total outsider, a mere acquaintance! Further, in his very presence, Lalita had deliberately called Girin aside and consulted him in low, intimate tones. Not so long ago, it was in the company of this very man that Shekhar had forbidden Lalita to pay a visit to the theatre!

At one point, Shekhar even tried to convince himself that Lalita had behaved in that manner with Girin out of embarrassment regarding her secret liaison with Shekhar—but, how could that be possible? If that were the case, would she not have attempted by some means or the other to speak to him about all these complicated issues that had come to pass?

Suddenly his mother's voice was heard outside, 'What is the matter, haven't you washed up as yet? It's getting on to be evening!'

Shekhar sat up in a rush, keeping his face averted at

such an angle as not to catch his mother's attention, and quickly proceeded with his evening ablutions.

These past few days his mind had continually pondered deeply on many matters; but there was one thing Shekhar had glossed over—whose fault was it really? Fully aware of the marriage plans for Lalita, he had not spoken even one word of reassurance to her, neither had he given her any opportunity to speak her mind. Rather, he had let himself die a thousand deaths in apprehension that she might make some untoward claims or revelations. He had marked Lalita as the perpetrator of all crimes and judged her harshly; at the same time, jealousy, rage, hurt and frustration were all but burning him to a cinder. This perhaps is the manner in which all men pass judgement, and this is how they are consumed inwardly by flames.

Shekhar had passed seven days burning in his own private hell when, one evening, a noise at the door made his heart beat wildly! Lalita, grasping Annakali firmly by the hand, entered his room and sat down on the carpet. Annakali said, 'Shekhar da, both of us have come to take leave of you. We are going away tomorrow.'

Shekhar stared at nothing in particular, left speechless by this sudden news.

Annakali continued, 'We have done you a lot of wrong, committed a lot of sins, please forgive it all.'

It was clear to Shekhar that these were not her words,

she was merely repeating what she had been taught. He asked, 'Where will you be going tomorrow?'

'To the west. All of us will be going to Munger with Baba—Girin Babu has a house there. We don't plan to return even after Baba's recovery. The doctor has said that climatic conditions here don't suit Baba.'

Shekhar asked, 'How is he now?'

'A little better.' Annakali took out some saris and showed them to Shekhar, saying Bhuvaneshwari had bought these for them.

Lalita had remained silent all this while. Getting up now and putting a key on the table she said, 'The key to the cupboard has been with me all this while.' Smiling a little she continued, 'But there is no money inside, everything has been spent.'

Shekhar said nothing to this.

Annakali said, 'Come along Lalita di, it is almost night.'

Before Lalita could respond, Shekhar hastily spoke up, 'Kali, just run below and fetch me some paan, won't you?'

Lalita caught Annakali's hand and said, 'You sit here Kali, I'll fetch it.' She went downstairs and returned with the paan which she gave to Annakali, who in turn handed them to Shekhar.

Shekhar sat in dumb silence, holding them in his hand.

'We'll have to leave now, Shekhar da,' Annakali said, respectfully bowing at his feet. Lalita bowed to the ground silently from where she was. Then both left the room slowly.

Shekhar sat there with his sense of propriety and pride intact; he sat in nonplussed silence, as though turned to stone. She had come, said what she had to—and left forever. But Shekhar had not been able to speak a word. The moment had passed by like he had no lines to speak at all. Lalita had deliberately brought Annakali with her to avoid any direct conversation with him——Shekhar was well aware of this. His entire being seemed to painfully come to life now; head spinning, Shekhar fell into bed with his eyes shut tight.

11

GURUCHARAN'S DETERIORATING HEALTH DID NOT MEND even in Munger. Within a year, casting away all earthly cares, he left for his heavenly abode. Girin had truly come to love him and till the very last nursed him to the best of his ability.

Before breathing his last, Gurucharan took both of Girin's hands in his own and, beseeching him never to sever ties with the family, requested him to let their deep friendship deepen further into a more intimate family bond. Failing health and rapidly passing time would not permit him to witness the happy occasion, but even from above, he would like to see the events come to pass. Girin, in utmost happiness and with all his heart, gave Gurucharan his word.

The tenants who had leased Gurucharan's house kept Bhuvaneshwari in touch with all that was happening to them; they conveyed the news of Gurucharan's demise to her.

Not much later, a momentous disaster took place in her own house. Nabin Roy passed away suddenly. Turning almost insane with sorrow and grief, Bhuvaneshwari headed for Benares, leaving the responsibility of the entire household to her daughter-in-law. She promised that she would return to solemnize Shekhar's marriage which was scheduled for the following year.

This match had been fixed by Nabin Roy himself and the wedding would have taken place much earlier, but his death had postponed matters for a year. But now, the bride's family did not want to delay things any further—and they had come the previous day and completed the engagement ceremony. The marriage was to take place that very month. Shekhar was getting ready to go and fetch his mother. As he brought out his things from the cupboard to pack, Lalita came to his mind after a very long while. All these chores used to be taken care of by her earlier.

It was over three years since Lalita and her family had left—for a long while there had been no news of them. He had made no effort to trace them either—probably there was no desire to do so. Gradually a kind of hatred had grown in his mind for Lalita. Today all of a sudden he wished he could find out how they all were by some means or the other. Of course, there was every reason for them to have prospered—Shekhar was quite aware that Girin was well to do; however, he wanted to know the details— when the marriage had been solemnized, how they all were—all that.

The tenants of Gurucharan's house were not there either—they had shifted elsewhere. Shekhar had once thought of approaching Charu's father—they would definitely have kept track of Girin's whereabouts. For some moments, putting aside the packing, he stared emptily through the window and brooded on these matters. Suddenly their elderly maid called aloud from outside the door, 'Chhoto Babu, Kali's mother would like to see you.'

In astonishment Shekhar turned around and asked, 'Which Kali's mother?'

The maid pointed out Gurucharan's house and said, 'Our Kali's mother, Chhoto Babu, they returned last night.'

'I'm coming,' Shekhar started out immediately.

The day was drawing to a close; no sooner had he stepped into the house than a loud keening resounded all around. Going near Gurucharan's wife who was clad in the garb of a widow, Shekhar sat down on the floor in front of her and silently swallowed his own tears. Sorrow, not just for Gurucharan, but for his own father as well, overwhelmed Shekhar all over again.

Lalita came into the room bearing lights when darkness had fallen all around. She greeted Shekhar from a distance and after waiting for a while left quietly. Shekhar could not bring himself to either look at or address this wife of another, a seventeen-year-old woman now. However a covert glance revealed a little, that Lalita had not just grown up, but had become a lot thinner too.

After weeping considerably, what Gurucharan's widow had to say amounted to this—all that she wanted to do now was to sell this house and live under the shelter of her son-in-law in Munger. Shekhar's father had craved to buy this house; now her family wanted to sell it to Shekhar's family for the right price. This way, they would feel that somehow they were still a part of it. They would not feel any trepidation about selling off the house and should they visit at any point of time in the future, she was sure that she'd be allowed to spend a few days there. Once Shekhar had reassured her that he would speak to his mother and do what he could, she wiped her tears dry and asked, 'Will Didi not pay us a visit now by any chance?'

Shekhar said that he was leaving that very night to fetch her. After that, Gurucharan's widow elicited other bits of information regarding the date of Shekhar's wedding, the amount of dowry the bride's family were offering, what jewellery had been bought, how Nabin Roy had passed away, how Bhuvaneshwari had coped with his death etc. etc.

When Shekhar was finally permitted to leave, the moon had risen. At the time, Girin was coming downstairs, and was probably going across to meet Charu's mother—his sister. Observing this, Gurucharan's widow asked, 'Shekharnath, are you not acquainted with my son-in-law? There is no one comparable to him anywhere in the world.'

Shekhar entertained no doubts about that at all; he said as much and also giving her to understand that he was acquainted with Girin, rapidly made an exit. But he was forced to come to a halt on entering the outer room.

In the darkness, Lalita was waiting behind the door. She asked, 'Are you going to fetch Ma tonight?'

Shekhar answered, 'Yes.'

'Is she very distressed?'

'Yes, she had all but turned insane with grief.'

'How is your own health?'

'I am well,' he said and left hastily.

Stepping out, Shekhar seemed to burn up in shame and disgust. It seemed to him that by standing in proximity with Lalita, he too had become sullied. On returning home he somehow managed to close his suitcase; knowing that there was still plenty of time before the train left, he stretched out on the bed and with the purpose of burning to a cinder Lalita's poisonous memories, fanned the flames of disgust all through his heart. In the agony of being seared through and through, he chided her in the harshest of terms; as a matter of fact, he did not even hesitate to call her a fallen woman. Then he recollected that Gurucharan's wife had said, 'That was a marriage of convenience, not joy—so, no one had been informed or invited, otherwise Lalita had said that your family ought to be intimated.' This sheer audacity of Lalita's seemed to ignite the flames of Shekhar's wrath even further.

12

WHEN SHEKHAR RETURNED WITH HIS MOTHER, THERE WAS still about a fortnight to go before his wedding.

A couple of days later, one morning, Lalita was sitting with Bhuvaneshwari and sorting and putting away some articles. Shekhar was not aware of this, and was startled when upon entering his mother's room, he found Lalita there. He stopped in his tracks. Lalita, with her head bowed, continued with the work.

His mother asked, 'What is it, dear?'

Having forgotten why he had wanted to meet her, Shekhar muttered a muffled 'No, let it be for now,' and quickly left the room. He had not caught a glimpse of Lalita's face, but his eyes had fallen on her hands. Though they were not completely bereft of ornaments, nothing other than a couple of glass bangles adorned each wrist. Laughing sardonically to himself, Shekhar scoffed at this hypocrisy. He knew that Girin was well to do and could think of no valid reason for his wife being virtually ornamentless.

That very evening as Shekhar was rushing downstairs on his way out Lalita was coming up the stairs. She immediately stepped aside, but, as he was about to pass, she spoke aloud, 'I have something to say.'

Stopping momentarily, in tones of amazement, Shekhar asked, 'To whom? Me?'

Just as gently Lalita continued, 'Yes, you.'

'What could you possibly have to say to me?' Shekhar made an even more rapid exit.

Lalita remained there in mute silence for a while and then releasing a little sigh, went her way.

Next morning Shekhar was sitting in the outer room and reading the newspaper when he looked up and saw, to his great amazement, Girin approaching. Greeting him, Girin pulled up a chair and seated himself. Returning the greeting, Shekhar put aside the newspaper and looked at him askance. While they had a nodding acquaintance, the two did not really know each other and neither had evinced any sort of desire to do so either.

Girin came to the point straightaway. He said, 'I have come to bother you on a certain matter of urgency. You know what my mother-in-law wants—to sell her house to your family. Today she has sent word through me to tell you that if the arrangements for the purchase of our house could be made soon, they could return this very month to Munger.'

Shekhar's mind was in a turmoil ever since he had set eyes on Girin and he did not care for the trend of the conversation at all. Somewhat gruffly he responded, 'All that is true, but in my father's absence it is Dada you will have to talk to.'

Responding with a pleasant smile Girin said, 'Yes, we know that too, but it would be the best if you approached him.'

Shekhar continued to respond in the same manner, 'It might work out if you talk to him too. You are now their guardian.'

Girin replied, 'If required I can do so, but Lalita di was mentioning yesterday that matters can be settled easily if you take a bit of trouble.'

All this while Shekhar had been leaning against a thick pillow for support. He suddenly sat up straight and asked, '*Who* was mentioning?'

'Lalita di. She was saying . . .'

Shekhar was absolutely dumbstruck with amazement. Not a word of what Girin said after this penetrated his ears. Staring at him in bewilderment he suddenly spoke aloud, 'Please forgive me, Girin Babu, but have you not married Lalita?'

Vastly embarrassed, Girin said, 'No, they all know . . . you . . . Kali and I . . .'

'But, that was not what was supposed to happen?'

Girin had come to know of everything from Lalita and said, 'It is true that that was not what had been planned. On his deathbed Gurucharan Babu had made me promise not to marry elsewhere. I too had given him my word. After his death, Lalita di explained to me—of course, nobody else knows all this—that she was already married and that her husband was alive. Perhaps someone else in my place might not have believed what she said, but I did not disbelieve a word. Besides, a lady cannot marry more than once, can she—whatever is the matter?'

Shekhar's eyes had misted over and now tears ran down his cheeks. But he was not even aware of them; it did not even occur to him that for a man to give vent to such a weakness in front of another man was not an accepted norm of how matters were conducted.

Girin stared at him in silence. He had had his own suspicions, now the identity of Lalita's husband was confirmed! Wiping dry his eyes, Shekhar asked in a thick voice, 'But, were you not very fond of Lalita?'

The reflection of some buried sorrow cast a shadow for a second on Girin's face, but at the next instance he began to laugh! Softly he said, 'It is unnecessary to answer that question. Besides, no matter what feelings might exist, nobody knowingly marries the wife of another. Please don't mind, I have no desire to discuss my elders in this manner.' Smiling once again Girin got up, 'Let me take my leave now, we will meet again.'

In his heart of hearts Shekhar had always felt a distaste for Girin, which had in the course of time grown into acute disgust. But that day when the young Brahmo boy left, Shekhar could not but offer his heartfelt respectful salutations. For the first time Shekhar had witnessed how a man can silently give up even the last vestiges of self interest, how one can keep one's word even in the most harsh and trying circumstances.

That evening, Bhuvaneshwari was sitting on the floor and with Lalita's help was sorting out the new clothes which were scattered all around in piles. Entering the room Shekhar seated himself on Bhuvaneshwari's bed. Today, he did not hurriedly leave on seeing Lalita. Looking towards him, his mother asked, 'What is the matter?'

Shekhar did not respond and continued to look at them silently. A little later he asked, 'What are you doing, Ma?'

'I am just trying to make a count of the people to whom the new clothes are to be distributed. Probably some more have to be bought, isn't it, dear?'

Lalita nodded in agreement.

Smiling, Shekhar asked, 'What if I do not marry?'

Bhuvaneshwari laughed, 'That you can do, you are more than capable of doing so!'

Shekhar too laughed, 'That is what might yet happen, Ma.'

His mother turned grave, 'What sort of talk is that? Do not talk in that inauspicious manner!'

'I have not spoken all this while, Ma, but it will be a grave sin if I continue to remain silent.'

Not following him, Bhuvaneshwari glanced at him in concern.

Shekhar said, 'You have forgiven your son a lot, Ma— pardon me this time too. Truly, I cannot marry that girl.'

Her son's words and demeanour truly concerned Bhuvaneshwari, but glossing over it she said, 'All right, it will be as you wish. Now go Shekhar, do not pester me—

I have a lot to do.'

Making another futile attempt to smile, Shekhar said in parched tones, 'No Ma, truly, this marriage cannot take place.'

'What is this childish behaviour all of a sudden?'

'It is not child's play, which is why I am saying all this, Ma.'

Now genuinely scared, Bhuvaneshwari said angrily, 'Explain to me, Shekhar, what this is all about! I do not like these complications.'

Mildly Shekhar responded, 'I will tell you another day, Ma, another time.'

'You will tell me another day!' Pushing aside the pile of clothes, Bhuvaneshwari said, 'Then, send me back to Benares today itself. I do not want to remain here even a moment longer under these circumstances.'

Shekhar sat in silence with bowed head. 'Lalita also wants to accompany me tomorrow,' Bhuvaneshwari said with even greater impatience. 'Let me see if she will be allowed to.'

Now Shekhar looked up with a smile, 'You will be taking her Ma, why do you have to ask permission for that from anybody? Who has more authority over her than you?'

Seeing a smile on her son's face Bhuvaneshwari was somewhat reassured. Looking towards Lalita she remarked, 'Did you hear what he said? He thinks I can take you wherever I please! Don't I have to ask her Mami for permission?'

Lalita did not answer. The trend the conversation was taking was making her feel acutely embarrassed and awkward.

Shekhar blurted out, 'If you want to inform her, do so by all means—that is as you wish. But whatever you say will be done, Ma. It isn't just me who thinks this way, but also the one whom you plan to take—she too feels the same way, for she is your daughter-in-law!'

Bhuvaneshwari was stunned. What manner of joke was this for a son to play on his mother! Staring at him fixedly she said, 'What did you say? What is she of mine?'

It was beyond Shekhar to raise his head, but he replied, 'Just what I said, Ma. This did not happen today, but four years ago—you are truly her mother. I cannot say any more; ask her Ma, she will tell you all.' Shekhar noticed that Lalita had got up and was respectfully bending down to touch his mother's feet; getting up, he stood beside her and both together completed this gesture, after which Shekhar silently left.

Tears of joy streamed down Bhuvaneshwari's face, she dearly and truly loved Lalita. Opening the almirah and taking out all her jewellery, she adorned Lalita in them with her own hands. Gradually she got all the information from Lalita. After listening to the entire account of what had happened, she asked, 'Is that why Girin married Kali?'

Lalita answered, 'Yes Ma, that is why. Whether there is someone else like Girin Babu in this world, I do not know. When I explained the situation to him, he immediately accepted the fact that I was married to another. Whether my husband acknowledged me or not was up to my husband, but he definitely existed and that was enough for Girin Babu to change his mind about marrying me.'

Bhuvaneshwari affectionately caressing her said, 'Of course your husband acknowledges you, my dear! May you both enjoy many, many years together. Just wait a moment, let me go and inform Abinash that the bride has been changed!' Smiling, Bhuvaneshwari moved away in the direction of her elder son's room.

IBD/18/08/05